## His kiss was warm, coaxing, and she clung to him

"Of all the senses touch is the most powerful," Simon murmured, pulling back a little. "Medical experiments—"

The words acted like a bucket of ice water. Anya's eyes widened, and she tore herself free, her cheeks flaming with shame and anger. Experiments?

What had possessed her? She'd been warned about Simon Brody, and she'd laughed. She'd said she was quite capable of taking care of herself—and here she was, off to a great start.

"Is that what all this is about?" she asked furiously. "A medical experiment?"

And while a part of her wanted to scrub at her swollen mouth with her handkerchief, another part of her knew that nothing would erase the memory of his kiss....

**Dana James** lives with her her husband and three children in a converted barn on the edge of a Cornish village. She has written thrillers, historical romances and doctor-nurse romances but is now concentrating her efforts on writing contemporary romance fiction. In addition to extensive researching, which she adores, the author tries to write for at least four hours every day.

## Books by Dana James

HARLEQUIN ROMANCE

2632—DESERT FLOWER
2841—THE MARATI LEGACY
2872—THE EAGLE AND THE SON
2926—TARIK'S MOUNTAIN

# Rough Waters

Dana James

Harlequin Books

TORONTO • NEW YORK • LONDON
AMSTERDAM • PARIS • SYDNEY • HAMBURG
STOCKHOLM • ATHENS • TOKYO • MILAN

Original hardcover edition published in 1986
by Mills & Boon Limited

ISBN 0-373-17031-9

Harlequin Romance first edition February 1989



Printed in U.S.A.

## CHAPTER ONE

THE crowded Star Ferry shouldered its way across the stretch of choppy water that separated Hong Kong Island from mainland Kowloon. Jostled by the pressing throng Dr Anya Lucas gazed out over the harbour, narrowing her eyes against the brilliant afternoon sun.

In front of her was Victoria, capital of Hong Kong, the modern blocks and skyscrapers gleaming in the sunlight, crowded together on a narrow flat strip much of which had been reclaimed from the sea. Behind the city reared steep rugged mountains over whose tree-covered slopes were scattered luxurious residences.

As her gaze swept forward Anya caught her breath, certain of a collision between the ferry and one of the hundreds of other craft on the busy strait.

Cargo boats, some smart in fresh paint, their flags of nationality snapping crisply in the breeze, others rust-streaked and filthy, chugged purposefully to and fro from jetties and loading bays. A sleek white passenger liner was being manoeuvred alongside the ocean terminal by busy tugs; her decks crowded with brightly clad sightseers anxious to leave their floating hotel and explore the colourful markets and alleys of this exotic, seething city.

Visiting warships were moored to large buoys in the centre of the outer harbour. Battered rowing boats and fragile sampans bobbed like eggshells on the wake of huge junks with eyes painted on their bows and powerful engines hidden in their scarred, shabby depths.

Suddenly, Anya's attention was caught by two navy-and-white police launches, sirens howling, as they wove at high speed through the confusion of boats, their creamy bow-waves flattening out to trail behind them in tangled ribbons of foam. They converged on an ancient-looking junk, its mud-coloured ribbed sail propelling it slowly towards Kowloon. It looked no different from dozens of others in the harbour. But within moments it was trapped between the launches and Anya heard the metallic bark of a tannoy. Uniformed figures carrying guns swiftly boarded the junk, manhandling the loudly protesting occupants with a roughness that startled her.

The ferry bustled on and though Anya leaned forward in an effort to see, the police and their captives were hidden by other craft. Conversation eddied around her and, above the nasal twang of Cantonese, a female American voice demanded, 'What kind of smugglers, Harry?' But Harry's reply was lost in the babble.

A bead of perspiration trickled down Anya's temple and she wiped it away, dabbing at her forehead and throat with a damp hanky. Her thin cotton shift clung stickily and discomfort pushed the incident from her mind.

Hot, moist air swirled through the open windows ruffling her hair, and automatically she raised her hand to the newly cropped style that had subdued her mane of cinnamon curls into a head-hugging feathery cap.

Once again she wondered at the impulse that had driven her into the expensive London salon. She had *always* worn her hair long, smoothing it back into a neat bun for her hospital duties. On her free days she had worn it loose, the rich tumbling tresses seeming almost too heavy for her slender neck.

What had prompted her to have it cut? Nigel hadn't liked the new look at all. 'Totally wrong for you,' he had announced, his brows knitted in a critical stare. 'Too sophisticated.'

Tact had never been Nigel's greatest asset. She had been on Casualty when Nigel had arrived as Senior Registrar in Orthopaedics. Their shared love of music had resulted in them attending several concerts together at the Royal Festival Hall and the hospital grapevine had buzzed with speculations as to the direction and development of the relationship.

But instead of their common interest in medicine drawing them together, it had in the end driven them apart. Nigel wanted nothing more than the security of a hospital consultancy, whereas she—well, what did she want? Anya had to admit she didn't know, only that whatever it was, it would not be found at Heathfield General, and certainly not as the wife of Nigel Bainbridge.

He had been more irritated than upset when she told him she was leaving to take a special course. An attitude which had bewildered her until she realised it was due to wounded pride rather than a broken heart.

'But why?' he kept asking. 'There must *be* a reason, though frankly I can't imagine what's come over you. First you chop off your hair, which you know I preferred long, now you're abandoning a safe position here for this harebrained idea of doing tropical medicine. *Tropical medicine?* What on earth is the matter with you?'

Anya had had no ready answer, only a sureness deep in her heart that what she was doing was right. She needed a complete change.

'I mean,' Nigel had persisted, 'what are people going to say?'

'Does it really matter?' Anya had asked gently. 'It's my life, my career, I'm not involving anyone else.'

'Yes, but I thought—everybody thought . . . You're simply being capricious, Anya, and I'm afraid your behaviour reinforces my opinion that women are inherently unstable. They have no place in medicine, except possibly as clerks or nurses.'

You pompous prig, Anya had wanted to shout at him, but she had clung grimly to her temper and now four months later and six thousand miles away from him, sniffing a breeze that carried with it the scent of frangipani blossom, and the pungency of woodsmoke, frying meat and incense, she could smile.

She was free, and on the threshold of a completely new life. Excitement tingled through her, bringing a sparkle to her emerald eyes, banishing the tiredness of the long journey.

It was amazing how everything had worked out. One of the lecturers supervising her short but intensive course had recently returned from Hong Kong. His description of the place and the medical problems of the people had fired Anya's imagination and instead of contacting one of the several private hospitals in the colony, she had applied to join the Floating Clinic Service, and to her joy had been accepted, her varied experience in Casualty being the deciding factor.

In a very short time she would be meeting her new boss, Simon Brody. From the brief correspondence they had exchanged it had not been easy for Anya to form a mental picture of the man responsible for running the several boats that made up the F.C.S. Every day the boats visited remote and inaccessible parts of Hong Kong and the New Territories where there were no doctors, no hospitals, in fact no medical care of any kind except that provided by the Service.

But if her previous contacts with administrators were anything to go by he would be short, plump and balding. He would wear dark suits and striped shirts and thick horn-rimmed glasses. His desk would be immaculately tidy but those of his secretary and clerks would groan under the weight of files and papers. At least one afternoon a week he would be unavailable as 'in conference' he discussed on-going budget problems with Department of Health representatives and tried to justify the previous year's overspending.

But above all he would be a theorist, directing operations from a comfortable office, never getting his hands dirty or his feet wet or seeing at first hand the problems faced by the people he was supposed to be helping.

Anya smiled wryly to herself. Bureaucrats were the same the world over.

The ferry drew alongside the dock and slinging the strap of her bag over her shoulder, Anya pulled her damply clinging dress from her midriff, picked up her suitcase and joined the throng surging towards the gangway.

The air-conditioned ferry terminal was a welcome respite from the afternoon heat and humidity.

After changing some money, Anya handed her suitcase to a baggage coolie. In the time it took her to reach the glass doors she overheard snatches of conversation in at least a dozen languages. But the sing-song cadences of the Chinese who outnumbered all the other nationalities made her acutely aware that her Cantonese was less than adequate for the job that lay ahead. Now she was actually here she could only hope she would quickly improve her accent and widen her vocabulary. At least she didn't have to learn to write it.

'Taxi, missy?' Without waiting for an answer the

coolie opened the door of a large, battered Ford, and with a broad grin revealing several gaps in his teeth, pocketed the two-dollar tip Anya gave him, bowed rapidly several times, and disappeared once more into the crowd.

'Des Voeux Road, please. The Gloucester Building,' Anya told the driver and sat back drinking in the view from the taxi window.

Even craning her neck she couldn't see the tops of the huge buildings lining the broad avenues of the central district. One huge department store proudly proclaimed its Victorian origins with decorated stonework, an ornate façade and wide doorways beneath a carved balustrade, provoking in Anya a sudden, unexpected pang of homesickness.

But as she stared at the shops the incredible richness and variety took her breath away. Modern units of glass and steel displayed Japanese cameras, videos, television sets and stereo units. Swiss watches and South African diamonds lay on midnight velvet beside creamy pearls, star sapphires and Chinese jade. There were alligator handbags and shoes of finest Argentine leather; Georgian silver, brass trays, copper lamps and crystal chandeliers; handwoven carpets from China, Turkey and Iran; Scandinavian ceramics, cosmetics from Paris, Alaskan furs, Scottish tweeds and cashmeres, Egyptian cotton and Thai silk; Indian ivory and chests of Borneo camphorwood. Anya couldn't absorb it all. There were so many people. They crowded the pavements, entering and leaving shops and offices, alighting from limousines, clambering on to buses.

Men in light-weight business suits; in blue, grey or black tunics with wide-legged trousers; in white shirts and blue jeans; in shorts and singlets; in the flowing robes of the Arab and the turban of the Sikh. Women in dresses, slacks, cheongsams and saris; with sleeping babies on their backs and almond-eyed toddlers at their knees; in plain cotton and shimmering silk, a kaleidoscope of colours and styles which merged and parted in an ever-changing pattern.

'Gloucester Building,' the driver said over his shoulder jerking her out of her reverie. Anya paid him and climbed out, the moist heat of the afternoon enveloping her like a blanket. She could only hope she would soon adjust to it. Picking up her suitcase she pushed open the nearest set of glass doors. Once again the air-conditioning provided instant and blessed relief. A huge board listing the offices and companies contained in the building directed her to the third floor.

Transferring her case to her left hand, she knocked briefly, opened the door and walked straight into the middle of a row. A tall, rangy man in faded jeans and a white T-shirt that clung damply to his heavily muscled shoulders was leaning on the receptionist's desk, his weight on both palms, his face dark with anger.

'And he still hasn't sent the requisition copies in?'

The fair-haired girl behind the desk shrugged helplessly. 'I reminded him again last night and he promised he'd drop them in today——' She broke off as they both noticed Anya who had paused just inside the door. The man straightened up, running an impatient hand through dark wavy hair, threaded with silver at the temples, that curled thickly on his neck, desperately in need of a cut. 'I'm sorry, Pam,' he muttered to the receptionist, 'it's not your fault. I'll go down and get them myself and read the riot act at the same time. I guess this has been——'

'—one of those days?' she finished for him and they exchanged a grin which for a fleeting instant totally altered his face, erasing the anger and frustration and revealing a self-mocking humour Anya would not have suspected.

Pam turned once more to Anya. 'Can I help you?'

'I'm Dr Lucas,' Anya explained, all too aware of the tall man's swift appraising glance as he looked up from a folder he had taken from the top of the filing cabinet. 'I believe Mr Brody is expecting me.'

'Oh, yes,' she replied and her quick, surprised smile puzzled Anya until the tall man slung the folder back on to the cabinet and took a step forward.

'I'm Simon Brody,' he announced, and Anya found herself staring into a pair of deep-set, tawny eyes as unblinking as a cat's. She recalled her imaginary picture of the man before her, now shattered into a million fragments. She automatically shook the hand he extended as, unable to help herself, she stammered, '*You're* Simon Brody, the F.C.S. Administrator?'

He nodded. 'It's Dr Brody, actually, I'm also Chief Physician and, as you probably guessed, chasing bits of paper is not an aspect of the job I particularly enjoy.'

'N-no,' Anya agreed dazedly.

'You're not quite what I expected,' he said bluntly, hooking his thumbs through the belt loops on his jeans as he studied her with a calm objectivity.

'Really?' she began crisply but he went on as if she hadn't spoken.

'I'm afraid I'm going to have to throw you in at the deep end. Let's hope you can acclimatise quickly. We have a particularly important job ahead of us this coming trip.'

Anya drew herself up, this kind of language she understood. 'I assure you, Dr Brody, I have no wish to waste either your time or my own. The sooner I can begin work the better. Now if you could recommend an hotel, just for a day or two until I can organise more permanent accommodation——'

'Excuse me for one moment,' he cut in, then turned to Pam who was watching them both with unconcealed interest. 'If Ned hasn't brought those requisitions in by six give me a ring at home and I'll deal with it.'

'Yes, Dr Brody. In the meantime would you like me to 'phone the Victoria or Mandarin hotels and book a room for Dr Lucas?' She was already reaching for the receiver.

'No, thank you, Pam.'

Her eyebrows lifted but he simply bent down and picked up a battered leather briefcase that bulged with files, then held out his hand. Without a word the receptionist passed him a large red-covered book which he squeezed into the case, fastening the straps. He turned to Anya, indicating her suitcase. 'Is that all your luggage?' When she said yes, he nodded approvingly and scooped it up without effort, the muscles in his bronzed arms and shoulders bunching beneath the thin cotton T-shirt. 'Right, let's go.' He glanced over his shoulder at the receptionist. 'I'll be at the Pharmacy by eight-thirty and on board by nine, so anything after that will have to wait. Have Carol and Susan confirmed their schedules?'

Pam nodded and made a note on her pad. 'By the way, Mr Ainsley called again from Government House, he wants to know if there was any chance of you getting to the Reception tomorrow.'

Simon frowned, 'Not another one. Call him in the morning and give him my apologies and tell him I'll contact him as soon as I get back. Is that the lot?'

Pam nodded, her fair hair swinging round her ears. 'Have a good trip.' Her smile grew speculative as she inclined her head towards Anya. 'Goodbye for now, Dr Lucas. *Bon voyage*.'

'Oh, yes, thank you,' Anya replied, slightly startled by Pam's choice of farewell. After all, the boats were only out for ten to twelve hours. She closed the office door and hurried after Simon who was striding towards the lift with her suitcase. The moist heat was like a weight on her head as she followed him on to the pavement. His raised hand and piercing whistle summoned a taxi to the kerb in seconds.

'Where are we going?' Anya asked as he got in behind her after putting her case in the boot.

'Peak tram terminal,' he instructed the driver, then sitting back he turned his head towards her and once again Anya was struck by the feral quality of his eyes, the strange gold flecks in them like splinters of sunlight. But it was the depth and steadiness of their gaze that unnerved her. 'To my house,' he replied calmly.

She was hot and tired. He had just warned her they had a particularly important job ahead of them and to be alert and ready to do all that would be required of her she needed a bath, a meal and a good rest. She certainly didn't feel like meeting his wife or his parents or whoever he lived with, and even less like making polite conversation. 'If you wouldn't mind, Dr Brody, I'd rather get my accommodation sorted out. It's been a long journey, and I did promise to contact a friend who works at the Queen Mary Hospital . . .'

'You hadn't planned to meet your friend tonight?'

'No,' she shook her head, 'I wasn't sure what time I'd arrive, so I was to 'phone tonight and arrange a meeting tomorrow.'

'Sorry, that won't be possible,' he said briefly.

'Oh? Why not?'

'Because we leave for the New Territories at nine tomorrow morning.'

'I beg your pardon?' Anya blurted. Had he said *we*?

'You and I, Dr Lucas, with two nurses, leave for a small settlement in the New Territories early tomorrow morning. I meant what I said about you going in at the deep end. I'm sorry but I really don't have any choice. The doctor who was to have accompanied me has gone sick and I can't take anyone off the other boats.'

That was reasonable. 'Yes,' Anya said slowly, 'I understand, but why are we going to your house?'

'Because there seems little point in paying for an hotel room you will not be occupying.'

'But—but—we'll be back tomorrow evening. Besides, I must unpack and leave my case and——'

'All of which you can do at my house,' he pointed out, turning away to stare out of the windscreen. 'And I'm afraid you're under a misapprehension, we won't be back tomorrow evening. The settlement we are going to is pretty remote and we're likely to be there for several days.'

'What?' Anya's head snapped round. 'But I thought—I mean—I understood——'

'Your mistaken impressions are not my concern, Dr Lucas.' He cut across her startled protest. 'If you wanted a nine-to-five job with all mod cons and the certainty of going home every night you should never have joined the F.C.S. I made it quite clear in my letter that the hours were flexible.'

Flexible was hardly the word, Anya thought crossly. There was quite a difference between twelve hours and the 'several days' he had sprung on her. Simon Brody had a conception of time that seemed elastic, to say the least.

He half-turned, his chin jutting and those strange tawny eyes narrowed and unblinking as he watched her. 'You do still want the job, I suppose?' His casual drawl didn't fool Anya, she heard the sardonic undertone, the trace of scepticism and recalled his earlier remark, 'You're not quite what I expected.'

It was on the tip of her tongue to ask him what he *had* expected but she held the words back. Her confusion had little to do with the conditions. It might take a while longer to adjust to the heat and humidity than she had imagined, and as for the trip lasting days instead of hours, well, that was all part of the challenge and excitement, the very reason she had chosen the Floating Clinic Service instead of the predictable security of a hospital. No, it wasn't the physical conditions that presented problems, it was . . .

'Well?' he demanded softly. 'Are you having second thoughts? You haven't signed the contract yet. If you're going to back out, now is the time to do it.'

'I have no intention of backing out, as you put it,' Anya retorted frostily. 'My work is important to me, Dr Brody. Uncertain hours and uncomfortable conditions are all part of the job. But as you said yourself, you are throwing me in at the deep end. Just give me a few minutes to get my bearings.'

He made a brief gesture with one hand and stared ahead once more. Out of the corner of her eye Anya could see his profile, black against the fading light, the hard determined lines of his forehead, nose and chin resembling something quarried from stone rather than warm living flesh. Only his mouth didn't fit the pattern. Instead of the thin, humourless gash one would expect, it was wide and full-lipped, the corners tilted upwards ever so slightly as if he were suppressing the urge to smile.

Anya looked away hastily. It wasn't the sudden change of plans that had thrown her, it was him. Nothing was the way she had imagined, least of all Simon Brody.

The taxi halted and within moments they were both on the funicular climbing steadily up the steep mountainside. So much was happening so quickly.

OK, so emergencies cropped up, people went off sick, extra duties were necessary. That she was prepared for but now Simon Brody was encroaching on other, private territory.

She had always been very possessive about the place she called home, whether it had been a room at whichever hospital she had been attached to, or the tiny flat she had left behind at Heathfield. It had been a secure haven from the pressure of work and a retreat from the social demands of her friends and colleagues. Nigel had complained, not altogether jokingly, about the rarity of invitations beyond the doorstep. She enjoyed company, but she was also quite happy to be alone. It was this ability to retreat into herself that sustained her in her highly demanding work on casualty.

But Simon Brody was threatening that security. She couldn't let him do that. Now more than ever she needed a place to call her own, if she was to adjust quickly to all that lay ahead.

'Don't you agree, Dr Lucas?' Simon Brody's voice murmured in her ear.

Anya started. 'I—I beg your pardon?' She spun round to face him, at once aware of the gleam of amusement in his eyes.

'The view,' he pointed, 'spectacular, isn't it?'

Automatically Anya turned to look, and caught her breath. To the west, beyond the purple hills of the New Territories, the sky shimmered pearl in pale memory of the fiery sunset which, deep in thought, she had missed, before darkening to turquoise, aquamarine, sapphire and indigo. Below her the city blazed. The orange glow of street lights strung out like necklaces was eclipsed by the screaming brilliance of a million neon lights. Whole apartment blocks were lit up like Christmas trees and the crowded sprawling city resembled a tangled skein of multi-coloured tinsel.

'Oh, it's beautiful,' Anya breathed and was suddenly flung against him as the cable car jolted to a halt.

'All right?' he sounded concerned.

'Fine.' She hastily jerked herself free of his steadying hand, busying herself with the strap of her bag which had fallen off her shoulder. She kept her head averted so he would not see her high colour. Her heart still thumped unevenly from the startling sensation of being pressed against his hard-muscled body from shoulder to knee. Her sharply indrawn breath had registered the warmth of his skin, his clean masculine smell tinged with the faintest trace of soap, was it cedar or sandalwood?

'Mind the step,' he said over his shoulder as he led the way out on to the road. 'It's not far. I imagine you're ready for a meal.'

Anya bit her lip. 'Look, Dr Brody, it's very kind of you but I don't think this is a good idea. I mean my turning up like this is going to cause a lot of inconvenience.'

He turned to look at her. 'For whom?' In the light of the street lamp she could see his eyes gleaming but the shadows across his face made his expression unreadable.

'Well,' Anya shrugged awkwardly, 'your wife, your family——'

'Here we are.' He put her case down on the pavement and unlocked the tall wrought iron gate set in a high wall. 'Please go ahead,' he gestured. Reluctantly Anya stepped inside and picking up her suitcase he followed, pausing only to close the gate and snap the padlock shut.

'You are hot inconveniencing me at all,' he said as they walked up the flagged path bordered on either side by shrubs and dwarf trees, 'and you have to agree this is the most logical solution under the circumstances.'

That was the trouble, Anya couldn't argue with the logic. They rounded a curve in the path and ahead of them was the house. Flanked by graceful willows, its red-tiled roof the colour of blood in the moonlight, the house exuded tranquillity.

'Oh, it's lovely,' she said aloud.

'And not what you expected.' Simon Brody unlocked the front door and switched on the light. Walking into the hall he dropped her suitcase and disappeared through a door on the right.

Had she really been that obvious? Anya hesitated on the doorstep, blinking as her eyes adjusted. The walls and ceiling of the hall were of palest green and the polished wood floor was almost completely covered by a large Chinese rug, its traditional design worked in cream and gold on to a jade background. In the corner to her left stood a long-necked vase painted dull gold containing pampas fronds. On her right, half-way down the hall past the open door through which Simon Brody had vanished, stood a small black laquered cabinet, its doors inlaid with ivory and mother-of-pearl. On it rested an exquisite figurine of a Chinese girl in a long pink dress and wide, fringed hat.

Beyond the cabinet a shallow staircase, with a jade carpet that matched the rug and a bannister of richly gleaming wood, swept round to the left, and out of sight. Below the curve of the staircase a darkened archway led, she assumed, to the rest of the ground floor.

Anya walked in and without thinking pushed the front door closed. Her preconceived notions were certainly taking a beating today. She would never have associated the sunburned, almost gipsy-like figure of Simon Brody with this subtle beauty. He had seemed much more of a smoked-glass and stainless steel, blonde leather and primary colours kind of person, modern, progressive. She certainly hadn't expected this traditional elegance with its almost tangible air of serenity. She could almost hear the silence.

Then it dawned. The locked gate, no lights, the way he had avoided answering her questions. She jumped as he re-entered the hall, this time without his briefcase. He scanned her face. 'Come now, Dr Lucas, what can I have done to deserve such an expression?' His voice was quietly mocking.

Anya flushed but held his gaze. 'Why didn't you tell me you lived alone?'

'You never asked. You spoke of inconveniencing my family. I assured you, quite truthfully, that you would not. Besides, I'm not alone, not quite.'

'I don't mean me,' Anya snapped.

'Nor do I,' he retorted, 'I have a housekeeper, but she lives in a flat over the garage. That way she retains her fiercely guarded independence and privacy, and I the illusion of being self-sufficient.'

'You mean you're not?' The question was out before Anya could stop it.

'Is anyone?' His amber eyes bored into hers. challenging, 'Are you?'

'I like to think so.'

He shrugged. 'Come on, I'll show you round. That's the study,' he indicated the room he had just left, 'and the kitchen is through the archway——'

'Dr Brody——' Anya began as he bent to pick up her suitcase, 'I think, if you don't mind——'

'But I do mind,' he cut in coolly. 'Dr Lucas, I don't know why you are so nervous, but I'd like to point out I'm not *asking* for anything, I'm trying to do you a favour. We have a lot of details to sort out before we leave tomorrow, and we are leaving early. You have had a long tiring day and so have I. Surely you see what a waste of time and money an hotel room would be when everything you need is right here, so what is the problem?'

He sounded so reasonable, so logical, Anya felt foolish, then angry. She had every right to be suspicious. She opened her mouth to tell him so but before she could speak he went on with the same quiet mockery, 'Also, while you are very attractive, I am not in the habit of leaping on women I hardly know, so should you be harbouring any such fears, do put them out of your mind and relax. If we are to be colleagues, Dr Lucas, we must have mutual trust, wouldn't you agree?' His knack of taking the wind out of her sails was intensely frustrating. It had been perfectly reasonable for her to feel the way she did, but with just a few well-chosen words he had reduced her to tongue-tied fury. Then the ridiculousness of the situation struck her and she had to fight the laughter that bubbled up inside her. Be honest, she told herself, you were worried that he might have ulterior motives. What are you going to do now, worry because he hasn't?

He touched the first door at the top of the stairs, 'Loo,' he said succinctly, 'the bathroom is next door.' As he started across the landing a telephone began ringing downstairs. 'Excuse me, I'll be back in a minute,' he took the stairs two at a time, 'next door along is yours, help yourself.' His voice floated up to her as he disappeared. The ringing stopped and Anya could hear his deep voice, but not the words. She hesitated, then opened the door nearest her.

She liked the room at once. Large and airy, it was almost spartan in its lack of ornament. The double bed was covered with an apricot and white spread at the head of which was a bookcase crammed with hardcover and paperback books. There was a large wardrobe of light oak and a matching chest of drawers with a mirror above it. A comfortable looking armchair stood in the alcove by the window. The walls were painted magnolia and there were tan rugs on the polished floor.

Anya put her bag on the chest and hauled her suitcase in from the landing. She unlocked it and had just thrown back the lid when two sandalled feet and a pair of blue jeans appeared in her line of vision. She straightened up quickly and saw amusement dancing in Simon Brody's eyes.

'Come with me.' He took her arm and led her across the landing. Opening the door he drew her gently in. 'Perhaps you'd be more comfortable in here.'

Anya glanced round. It was indeed pretty, all rose-pink and ivory. 'It's very nice,' Anya agreed, 'but I don't want to put you to any trouble, and I'm quite happy with the other room.'

'I'm glad to hear that, Dr Lucas,' his face was expressionless, 'but if you stay there you might have trouble sleeping.'

'The bed felt fine——'

'Oh, it is. But I'll be in it. You see, that's my room.'

Anya, flustered, bit the inside of her lip. 'I'll just get my bag——'

'And I'll bring your case. There are fresh towels in the bathroom. As soon as you've showered come on down, I'll have some food ready.'

Her thoughts buzzing like a swarm of bees, Anya bathed and changed into a caftan patterned in different shades of green with a gold thread running through it. The crinkle cotton was cool against her skin, falling loosely from a square neckline, the full sleeves gathered on to a buttoned band at each wrist.

She pulled a comb through her still-damp hair, the

coppery curls feathering on her forehead and neck. Her skin glowed dewy-fresh from the shower and the colour of her dress emphasised her emerald eyes under their thick lashes. Critical of her generous mouth and wide cheekbones Anya decided against make-up. This was not exactly a social occasion and Simon Brody had made it quite clear he was only interested in her professional abilities.

Later, Anya lay in bed and thought back over the evening. The meal had been delicious, cold chicken, rice and peppers with a spicy sauce of pineapple, mango, ginger and lemon served with a crisp green salad. A dessert of lychees had been followed by freshly percolated coffee. The food had started to relax her but it had been Simon Brody's conversation that had completed the job. He had broken the ice by encouraging her to talk about her work at Heathfield. Then he had outlined the work of the clinic boats and recounted some funny and frightening incidents he had been involved in. Soon she had been utterly absorbed, leaning forward, her elbows on the table, chin resting on her clasped hands as she listened, excitement stirring in her at the thought that she was now a part of it, that the following day she, too, would be setting out on one of the boats for a remote destination to bring comfort and help to people who desperately needed it.

She snuggled into the pillow. Simon had been right—Simon, his name sounded strange on her lips. It had been his idea that they switch to first names, it made for a better working relationship, he had said. Though administratively he was her boss, on the boat they would be working very much together, sharing duties and responsibilities. To have retained titles would have created a barrier to her smooth integration into the team.

Anya smiled sleepily. Simon has been right, this was far better than staying at an hotel. No doubt her friends would be surprised—she shot upright in bed. Charles! She had promised to 'phone him as soon as she arrived. She had forgotten all about it. Snapping on the light Anya peered at her watch. It was almost eleven. Should she try to reach him now? It was rather late. But there would be no time in the morning.

She slipped out of bed and pulling her cotton dressing gown on over her nightie, padded downstairs. Light showed under the door of Simon's study.

Anya tapped on the oak panels and opened the door. He was sitting at a large desk, his back to the curtained window, with several folders open in front of him.

He looked momentarily startled then a strange light brightened his eyes.

'I'm sorry to bother you,' Anya said quickly, automatically tugging the thin cotton around her more tightly, 'but I promised to 'phone a friend when I arrived and it completely slipped my mind.' He raised one dark brow and she blushed. 'I—I wondered if I might do it now?'

He pushed back his chair and stood up, indicating the telephone on his desk. 'Go ahead. Do you have the number?'

Anya nodded, holding up her small address book, only too aware that it had been due to Simon Brody's impact on her that she had forgotten Charles. The knowledge flooded her face with colour. 'Please don't let me disturb you.' She was deliberately formal. 'I can use the 'phone in the kitchen.'

He shook his head, then yawned and stretched and she could not help but be aware of the power in his tall, muscular body. 'I'm about finished anyway.' He pushed both hands through his thick hair rumpling it even more, then flexing his shoulders he came round the desk towards her, his eyes gleaming like a cat's in the light from the desk lamp. She held her ground and her breath, but he stopped an arm's length away. 'Sleep well, Anya.'

'And you—Simon.' Anya managed, feeling the warmth in her cheeks as his glance flickered over her. Then he was gone, a smile curving his mouth as he closed the door behind him.

Anya leaned against the desk, clasping the receiver tightly while she dialled the number, aware of her heart's uneven thump as she forced the memory of that smile out of her mind. Damn Simon Brody. She was a grown woman yet he could make her feel as gauche and awkward as a schoolgirl. 'Hello? Charles? It's Anya—yes, I know it's late—no, I'm fine—no, no problems at all, just a change of arrangements that rather complicated things.' That was putting it mildly, she thought to herself. 'I'm not in an hotel actually. No, I'm staying at Dr Brody's house—yes, of course he's here too——' Anya listened for several seconds, a deepening frown creasing her forehead. 'No, I don't think it's a damn-fool thing to do. As a matter of fact it's extremely sensible as we are leaving for the New Territories first thing in the morning.' What an about face, now she was trying to convince Charles with the very words Simon had used to convince her. There was another pause then, 'I'm not sure,' she said, 'several days, I believe. Of course, I'll 'phone as soon as we get back.' She shifted her weight to her other foot. 'I was looking forward to it as well, but—yes, I'll take care. You, too.' She listened again, twisting the sash of her robe around her finger, stiffening as her exasperation mounted. 'For heaven's sake, Charles,' she burst out at last. 'I'm a big girl now. I can take care of myself—yes, I'll remember. See you soon. Bye.'

Anya replaced the receiver thoughtfully. 'Just watch your step,' Charles had warned, 'Simon Brody has quite a reputation. He eats girls like you for breakfast, but none of them ever held him.'

Chin high, Anya marched back upstairs. She should have told Charles, her new job would absorb all her time and energy. Simon Brody's reputation was no concern of hers.

## CHAPTER TWO

ANYA was woken from a restless sleep by staccato rapping on the door. 'Don't let me rush you,' Simon's voice came clearly through the thick oak, 'but we leave in twenty minutes.'

'I'm on my way,' she croaked, stumbling out of bed. Ten minutes later, after a quick shower and a hurried rake with the hairbrush, Anya flew down the stairs, cross with herself for being late on her first morning.

Taking her cue from Simon's ultra-casual clothes the previous day, Anya had pushed her skirts aside and decided on a short-sleeved blouse in tan cotton and matching trousers. Low-heeled sandals completed her cool, practical outfit.

As she reached the bottom of the stairs he passed her heading for his study. He had on the blue shirt he'd worn the previous night and a clean but faded pair of jeans outlined his long, powerful legs.

His swift glance scanned her from head to toe. 'There's fruit and rolls, coffee's in the jug,' he said briskly. 'Come to my study as soon as you've eaten,' and before she had the chance to say a word he strode past, leaving behind him the fresh tang of the soap he had used.

There was a strange sensation behind her ribs as Anya watched his tall figure disappear into the study. She gave herself a mental shake and hurried into the kitchen to eat her breakfast, standing by the window, and looking down over the lush green mountainside to the concrete and glass of the central district, heart of Hong Kong's world-wide financial network. The waters of the strait, already bustling with traffic, sparkled in the early morning sun. From the speed at which clouds were moving across an intensely blue sky, Anya could tell that the breeze rustling the willows outside her bedroom window was going to become much stronger. She had a moment's misgiving. Just how rough would the water be? It was impossible to judge from up here. She banished the thought, swallowing the last of her coffee. She'd be finding out soon enough and until she did, what was the point of worrying?

As she entered the study Simon was leaning over the massive desk sorting some papers. She had gathered only a fleeting impression of the room the previous evening; dark wood, rich leather and masses of books, a totally masculine environment. The warm sunshine did nothing to dispel that impression. Yet it was comfortable and not in the least intimidating and would, Anya sensed, be marvellous to work in. How different from her tiny flat where many of her beloved books had had to remain in boxes because there were simply not enough shelves to take even half of them. But a room like this . . . Careful, a little voice warned, don't get carried away. Your staying here is a purely temporary arrangement, and all your work will be done either on board the clinic boat or ashore.

Simon looked up as she walked towards him. 'Right, first things first.' He pushed two sheets of thick, headed paper covered in close typing towards her. 'Your contract. There's also a special medical insurance. We operate a private scheme to cover illness or accident at sea.'

Anya picked up the top sheet. He seemed different this morning, more distant. She wondered what had caused the change, then gave a mental shrug. Doubtless he had a lot on his mind, and in any case it was really no concern of hers.

Taking the pen he offered, she bent over the desk. As the nib touched the paper, he warned, 'This isn't an easy job and it can sometimes be dangerous. Once you sign you are committed, there'll be no backing out. You might be the first woman doctor in the F.C.S. . .'

Anya looked up quickly. She hadn't known that, not that it made the slightest difference, except that she didn't want to be looked on as an experiment or a special case. His next words reassured her on that point, '. . . but you'll get no preferential treatment.'

'I don't expect it,' she replied coolly, and signed the two documents firmly. She handed back his pen and watched as he added his own name in a bold scrawl. Then he placed the papers in the top drawer of his desk and locked it. 'I'll give you your copy when we get back.' He held out his right hand with a grin that crinkled the corners of his eyes and revealed white, even teeth. 'Welcome to the Floating Clinic Service, Anya.' The grin twisted slightly, becoming sardonic. 'I wonder if you have any idea what you've let yourself in for.'

She took his hand, unprepared for the sensation that tingled through her, constricting her throat and bringing a swift flush to her cheeks. 'Well,' she said brightly, almost snatching her hand free and fervently hoping he hadn't noticed, 'I guess I'm about to find out.'

'Right, collect your bag and we'll get moving.' He glanced at his watch and his dark brows formed a bar as he frowned. 'We're already running late.'

Anya managed to stifle her gasp. An overnight bag, she'd forgotten all about that. 'I'll only be a moment,' she said and raced for the stairs.

'I hope you've kept it light,' he shouted after her, 'stowage space is limited and we don't change for dinner.'

Anya pulled a face, then bursting into her room, dragged her case from under the bed and pulled out the foldaway tote bag. Throwing in her toilet bag and a towel, she scrabbled in the top drawer of the dressing table for spare bra and pants then, yanking open the wardrobe, she grabbed a pair of green cotton trousers and a yellow T-shirt and stuffed them in. Snatching her thin cotton robe off the bed as an afterthought she rolled it up, pushed it into the bag and slamming the door shut, sprinted down the stairs, zipping the bag as she went.

She reached the hall and almost knocked over a tiny Chinese woman coming from the kitchen. Her face was as brown and wrinkled as a walnut but her black eyes were as bright as a bird's, twinkling like two boot buttons beneath papery lids. Her grey hair was drawn back in a neat bun and she was wearing a beige cotton tunic with wide sleeves, baggy black trousers and black canvas sneakers.

'I'm terribly sorry,' Anya apologised and the little woman at once tucked her hands in her sleeves and bowed as Simon Brody appeared behind her.

'. . . and don't tidy my desk,' he was saying, 'the last time you did that I couldn't find anything for weeks.' He slipped an arm around the old woman's shoulders. She was as small as a child beside him. 'Ah Mai, this is Dr Lucas. She's in Kerry's room.'

'How you do, Missy Yucas,' Ah Mai enunciated carefully, and bowed again.

Anya hesitated, unsure whether to offer her hand. Instead she smiled and inclined her head. 'I'm happy to meet you, Ah Mai.' But who was Kerry?

Introductions over, Simon turned to the little woman, dropping his arm. 'I'm hoping we'll be back by Friday, but in case we're delayed, leave something cold in the fridge.'

*'Dor jeh,'* Ah Mai nodded. Then she grinned up at him, wrinkling her nose as she covered her mouth with one hand. *'Ying gock yun gwai lo ho lan,'* she murmured, her black eyes dancing as she peeped from one to the other.

Anya smothered a grin as she brushed some non-existent dust off the front of her trousers, half-embarrassed, half-amused. She had never been called an English foreign devil before, neither had she ever heard herself described as beautiful. She couldn't resist a side-long glance at Simon Brody.

His face darkened. *'Jaow hoy, hui,'* he pointed towards the kitchen. Ah Mai went, still chortling, not in the least put out, and Simon lowered his head towards Anya.

'Do you think we might get to work sometime this morning?'

She flushed and taking a firm grip on the tote-bag, started towards the front door. As she reached it with him close behind, the 'phone started ringing.

'Damn,' he muttered explosively and Anya turned to see him scowling at his watch. Just then Ah Mai trotted out of the kitchen, waving her hands in excitement. 'Missy Kerry, she call from Swisserland, you talk?'

Simon Brody's frown dissolved into a delighted smile. 'Of course I'll talk, ask her to hold on.' He thrust his briefcase at Anya. 'I don't know how long this will take, you'd better go on ahead. The Pharmacy is in the Gloucester Building, turn left instead of right when you leave the elevator. Check the order against the blue copy in the requisition book, it's in this case.'

'Are the supplies to go to the boat?' Anya asked quickly.

'You wait for me. Now get going.'

'I'd better get my purse, I'll need money for fares and——'

He dug into his jeans' pocket, pulled out a handful of notes and coins, slapped them into her hand and gave her a non-too-gentle push. 'I'll meet you at the Pharmacy.' As the front door closed she heard him call, 'I'll take it in my study, Ah Mai,' and determinedly ignored the pang in the region of her heart.

Indigestion, she told herself fiercely as she hurried along the road to the cable car, that's what came of bolting her breakfast. Jealousy? That was ridiculous. How could it possibly be? She had known him less than twenty-four hours, and he had made it very clear that his interest in her was purely professional. But why was he so distant, almost formal, when yesterday . . .

He had yelled at Pam over the requisitions, but had apologised at once and they had laughed together. Ah Mai obviously had him round her little finger. And Kerry? She had to be very special if he could so easily abandon his tight schedule, and do so with a smile that would melt a glacier.

Pull yourself together, she admonished. You're an unknown quantity as far as he's concerned. It's up to you to prove your capability, after all that's what you are here for, to work.

When Anya opened the door, she wondered for a moment if she was in the right place. A Chinese girl receptionist sat behind a layered screen of toughened glass.

'This is the Pharmacy?'

'May I have your name, please?' was the girl's reply.

'Lucas, Dr Anya Lucas. I've come to collect a drug and medical supplies order for the F.C.S.'

'One moment, please.' The girl smiled politely and pressed a button on an intercom, leaning forward to speak a few words. The brief, crackling reply must have satisfied her for she reached under the desk and with a metallic clunk that made Anya jump, the heavy wood and metal door to her left opened a fraction. 'Please go through,' the girl instructed. 'You are expected.'

Anya closed the door behind her and it locked automatically. She had only seen security precautions like those in banks, but there wasn't time to ponder the reasons. Reaching the first door at the end of the passage, she raised her hand to knock, but before her knuckles touched the wood it opened and a middle-aged Chinese in a white coat and gold-rimmed glasses beamed at her. 'Dr Lucas? I am Robert Han, Dispensing Pharmacist, please come in.'

The shelves, from floor to ceiling, were stacked with jars, bottles and boxes. Two more bays, also laden, ran parallel down the centre of the long room. Opposite her, beneath windows screened by half-closed venetian blinds, was a wide, formica-topped counter. It, too, was piled high with packets of lint, boxes of dressings, and sealed rolls of gauze and cotton wool. Two young men in white coats were busy at the shelves, one re-stocking from a huge loaded trolley; the other, armed with a clipboard to which were attached several white flimsy sheets, was working his way down the bays collecting items and placing them in another trolley.

'Your order is all ready.' He beckoned one of the young men over. 'Now Dr Lucas is here, you can fetch that special vaccine from the refrigerator.' The young man nodded and hurried away. Robert Han gestured towards a neatly stacked mound of boxes, packets, and bottles. 'It is Dr Brody's policy to check the order before it leaves the premises, so please use the counter. I hope you will forgive my not staying, but there are gentlemen from two leading drug companies waiting to see me.'

'No, of course,' Anya said, then a slight frown appeared between her brows. 'Mr Han,' he turned at the door, 'does Dr Brody always leave interviews with drug reps to you?'

'Dr Brody is an extremely busy man,' Robert Han replied, his smile fading. 'It is my pleasure and privilege to relieve him of some of the less demanding tasks. Goodbye, Dr Lucas.'

That's telling me, Anya thought wryly. The young man had returned with a large flat insulated box, and now hovered at her shoulder. Anya took it from him. 'Please carry on with whatever you were doing,' she smiled, 'I'll check this lot and pack as I go. Can I use those large cartons?'

He nodded, blushing, and disappeared among the shelves.

Anya glanced at her watch. Simon should be arriving at any moment. She pulled the requisitions book from the briefcase and began to work. It took her almost thirty minutes to check the order and pack the boxes. She returned the book to the case and looked at her watch again. Where was he? What on earth could be keeping him? Surely a 'phone call couldn't take that long?

Hanging about like this was ridiculous. It would be far more sensible to take the consignment down to Simon's boat and get it unpacked. At least she'd be doing something useful. Besides, that vaccine should be put under refrigeration again as soon as possible. 'Is there a 'phone I might use?' she asked the nearer of the two technicians.

'Su-yin has outside line,' he stammered, colouring.

Thanking him she went down the corridor. Su-yin's little glass cage was empty, so Anya looked up Simon Brody's number in the directory. Ah Mai answered. No, Dr Brody was not at home, he had left some time ago. Anya jabbed the receiver rest with her finger. Then where was he? Why hadn't he arrived? Wait, he'd said, but for how long? She hesitated, then decided to act. There was a list of taxi numbers on a card beside the 'phone. Anya dialled the first one and ordered a cab. Then she went back to the stockroom, found an empty trolley and loaded the cartons into it. The technicians watched her, exchanging glances. She put the last box into the trolley, laid her bag and the briefcase on top, and beckoned the nearer of the two. 'When Mr Han is free would you please tell him I've taken Dr Brody's consignment down to the dock. Perhaps Mr Han would inform Dr Brody when he arrives.' If he ever does, she added under her breath. The young man nodded uneasily, and was on the verge of saying something but changed his mind.

Anya pressed the button under Su-yin's desk to unlock the door then, pushing the trolley ahead of her, marched down the passage to the lift. Luckily there was only one other passenger, for the trolley took up a lot of room, and he eyed her suspiciously, but Anya ignored him, fully occupied with her own thoughts.

The taxi was waiting outside as she manoeuvred the trolley down the step. The driver did a double-take when he saw the cartons, some labelled with the names of drug companies. He leapt out of his seat and rushed round to where Anya was struggling to push her bag and the briefcase on to the floor at the far side of the cab.

'You got no man with you?' he demanded, glancing repeatedly over his shoulder at passers-by.

'I should have thought that was obvious,' Anya panted, heaving in another box. 'You know where I want to go? Queen's Pier, the F.C.S. dock.' She lifted another box on to the seat then took the last two out of the trolley and put them on the pavement while she tried to make more room in the cab. 'If it's not too much trouble,' she said sweetly, 'would you push the trolley back into the foyer?'

The driver grew even more agitated, glancing left and right, plainly nervous. 'You hurry, lady. No good hang about.' He grabbed the trolley and barged across the pavement with it, heedless of the annoyed pedestrians.

What on earth was the matter with these men? Anya heaved the last box on to the seat. First the technicians, now the driver. None had offered to help, and their behaviour was quite odd. The driver skittered round the bonnet, jumped into the driving seat and started the engine, revving it continuously.

Anya was about to get in when a hand grasped her shoulder and she was jerked around. Simon Brody glowered down at her, eyes blazing in a face taut with barely controlled fury. 'What in God's name do you think you are doing?'

Anya sighed with relief, her heart thudding painfully. 'Oh, you frightened me,' she gasped.

'Frightened you?' His voice was a low hiss. 'Woman, I haven't even started. What are you doing out here?'

The relief melted, trickled away, and was replaced by anger. 'Isn't it obvious? I'm taking the consignment to the dock——'

His grip was savage, biting into her shoulder with such force she nearly cried out. 'You alone? With six boxes of medical supplies including narcotic drugs, unguarded in a taxi? Are you insane?'

His anger was terrifying. Bewilderment and alarm swept her own anger aside. 'I—I don't understand. What's wrong? I——'

'Shut up,' he snarled and bundled her into the cab, climbing in after her, mercilessly crushing her against the boxes as he leaned forward and spoke to the driver in rapid Cantonese. The taxi surged forward and Simon swung round, his legs jammed against hers in the confined space.

'You disobeyed an order.' His eyes were tiger-bright. 'I told you to wait.'

'I did wait,' Anya flung back, 'over an hour. You were the one who was worried about being late. I was trying to save time, I thought it would help.'

'Thought,' he spat, 'you didn't think at all. Do you know where you are? This is Hong Kong, not some English market town. Kowloon City is only minutes from here through the cross-harbour tunnel. Do you know what's special about it? It is totally free from any political or judicial authority. It is a refuge for every criminal and drug-trafficker in the Colony.' Anya flinched as he brought his head down. 'Do you have any idea what that lot would fetch on the black market? And what do you think they'd do to you?' He wrenched himself away from her, staring out of the window as he wiped the beads of perspiration from his forehead, then ran an unsteady hand through his thick, dark hair.

Anya's mouth was paper-dry as the risk she had run began to sink in. He glanced at her again, and as their eyes met she could see the fury beginning to evaporate and he had himself once more completely under control. 'Didn't the security precautions register at all?' he demanded tightly. 'Didn't it occur to you there must be a reason for them?' He didn't wait for her reply. 'We use a service entrance in a protected courtyard at the back of the building to load and unload supplies. There is also a special service elevator with a combination lock, and we have special vans to make deliveries to the dock, and none of us ever, *ever* travels alone.'

Anya swallowed. 'Why didn't the technicians stop me?'

'How could they? You outranked them and no doubt they thought you were acting on my authority.'

They both fell silent and a few minutes later arrived at the dock. A sudden heavy shower had left the air even steamier despite the stiff breeze as Anya clambered out of the taxi after Simon.

His piercing whistle quickly summoned two crewmen from the boat moored to the quay and under Simon's direction they quickly unloaded the boxes, carrying them on to the boat while he paid off the driver, who roared away in a cloud of exhaust, seeming to Anya keen to put as much distance as possible between himself and the crazy Englishwoman.

She looked at the boat. It was about fifty feet long. Its white superstructure, painted with a large red cross above the initials F.C.S., gleamed in the brilliant sunshine, but the black hull was scarred and scratched despite the fenders along the side.

'Are the nurses on board?' Simon asked one of the crewmen and when he nodded went on, 'Then tell the skipper we're ready to go. By the way, what's the forecast?'

The crewman flicked a sideways glance at Anya before he replied carefully, 'Not so good, Doctor.'

Simon frowned then shrugged. Turning to Anya he said briskly, 'Come on, we've got a lot to do,' and leaping down from the dock on to the grey-painted deck, he held out his arms, 'Bags first.'

Anya tossed down her tote-bag and his briefcase. He caught them smoothly and set them down then as she hesitated called impatiently, 'Jump, woman, it's only a few feet.'

Anya jumped, but her right foot landed on the corner of the briefcase and twisted, throwing her forward into Simon's arms with a force that knocked her breathless. She was aware of the hardness of his chest and the strength in his deeply tanned arms as he set her on her feet again, releasing her quickly.

'Sorry——' she began, but he was already picking up the bags.

'Heaven help us.' He eyed her over his shoulder. 'It's flat calm and you're falling about already. What are you going to be like at sea?' He led the way below.

Anya looked over the side at the short, choppy waves as the crew cast off and the boat began to swing her bow round as they moved out into the strait, heading east towards the Lyemun Pass. She wouldn't have called this a flat calm, as far as she was concerned it looked quite rough, despite the bright sunshine.

'There's nothing wrong with my balance,' Anya retorted, 'I caught my foot——'

'Of course,' he cut in, but it was obvious from his tone that he didn't believe her.

She glared at his broad back. She would not argue, it wasn't worth it. She knew the truth, if he chose to believe otherwise . . .

He turned. 'This first door on the left is the nurses' cabin, next to that are the showers and loo, referred to on board as the heads. Beyond is the saloon where we have our meals, then there's the galley and in the bows the crew's mess and their quarters. They have their own showers, etcetera. Here on the right,' he opened the first door, 'is where you'll be sleeping.' Anya peered round the door. Though the cabin was tiny it contained two bunks set at right angles to one another. Lockers stood at the foot of one bunk and the head of the other and there was a wardrobe behind the door, all of which left a space only two feet wide and six feet long to move about in. Still, it was neat and compact, and after all, how much room did she need?

'Leave your bag,' Simon ordered, 'you can unpack later. I'll show you the medical facilities now. No, that one.' He pointed to the narrower of the two bunks, its head beneath one of the portholes, its foot towards the inner wall. Anya didn't have time to ask why before he disappeared down the passage and she had to hurry to catch up with him.

'This next door is the consulting room.' He opened it and walked in. The narrow room was just big enough for a desk, a filing cabinet, two chairs and an examination couch on which stood three of the cartons from the Pharmacy. 'Which leads on the right into our dispensary—remind me to give you a set of keys—and the double doors on the left go through to the operating theatre. This is the biggest boat in the F.C.S. at the moment and the first with facilities to do overnight trips.'

Through her feet Anya could feel the vibration of the engines and the slight pitch and roll as the boat got properly under way. It wasn't enough to make her stagger or clutch at something for support, but she was aware of the muscles in her legs responding to the constant movement of the floor beneath her feet. Flat calm, he'd said, and this was the largest boat. What on earth would it be like . . .?

The operating theatre doors opened and two nurses wearing white uniform dresses and white canvas shoes but no caps came into the consulting room. Anya judged them both to be a couple of years younger than herself. The first was plump with straight black hair cut in a neat bob with a fringe. Her round face was unmistakably Chinese and after a moment's surprised hesitation as she saw Anya, she beamed a cheerful smile at them both.

'Morning, Susan,' Simon greeted her.

'Good morning, Dr Brody.' Her voice was quite high-pitched, but her English had hardly a trace of accent.

'Susan, this is Dr Anya Lucas, our newest recruit to the F.C.S. Anya, this is Nurse Susan Chang, who specialises in midwifery and child care.'

Anya held out her hand. 'Good morning, Nurse Chang. I hope I can count on your help and advice. No doubt the patients will be rather wary of me to begin with, and I'm sure your background and experience will make things easier for both them and me.'

The nurse flushed with surprise and pleasure. 'But of course, Dr Lucas.'

'And this is Nurse Carol West.' Simon smiled at the other girl. 'She has only been with us six months, but has proved invaluable in theatre.'

Anya held out her hand once more. 'I'm happy to meet you, Nurse West. Before coming out here I was Casualty Officer at a large London hospital . . .' how long ago that seemed, '. . . and I know how vital an efficiently run theatre was to the speed and success of our operations. I'm sure that applies even more out here with the limited facilities and very difficult conditions.'

Carol West's face lit up for a moment. 'Thank you, Dr Lucas. I hope you'll find everything satisfactory.' But her smile faded quickly and Anya noticed how pale and drawn she looked. Perhaps it was the combination of white uniform, fair skin devoid of make-up and her light, almost ash blonde hair which she wore in a pony-tail curled under and secured with two grips. She appeared to be very slim as well, but Anya knew how deceptive that could be. At Heathfield the skinniest nurses had often turned out to be the wiriest and toughest, with reserves of strength and energy their more well-upholstered colleagues could only envy.

'How far have you got?' Simon asked as soon as the introductions were over.

'We're preparing dressing packs,' Susan answered. 'The autoclave is working well now. I tested the thermostat and it is registering accurately.'

'Fine.' He nodded. 'Carry on. Carol, the new scalpel blades have arrived, so you can fit those and start sterilising instruments when you're ready. Dr Lucas and I will unpack the drugs.'

'What about the valves and pressure gauges on the oxygen and nitrous oxide cylinders?' Carol sounded brisk and matter-of-fact but Anya sensed it was costing her a lot of effort.

'I'll be in in just a minute,' Simon promised and both nurses disappeared into the theatre, the doors swishing closed behind them.

Anya was curious. 'What's the matter with the valves?'

'Heat and humidity.' He grimaced. 'I keep the air-conditioning on permanently, but they still stick and, as having patients turning blue from anoxia or waking up in the middle of operations could be inconvenient, I test and check the valves and gauges at the beginning of every trip as well as before each operation. After you.' He opened the door and switched on the two overhead lights then stood back to allow Anya to precede him into the dispensary. It was a little more than a walk-in cupboard, about six feet wide and seven feet six inches long.

She looked around. There were no portholes. Security again, she thought. Waist-high cupboards with sliding doors were topped with white formica. Above the work-tops shelves reached to the ceiling.

Several books, an angle-poise lamp, two measuring jars and a tablet counter lay on the left hand work-top, and at the far end of the room stood a tall cupboard with double doors and next to that a refrigerator. The air-conditioning whirred softly.

Anya glanced over her shoulder as Simon carried in one of the cartons on top of which was balanced the insulated container.

'Put that in the fridge right away, will you, near the bottom.' He nodded at the container as he put the box on the counter and went to fetch another.

'What is it?' Anya opened the fridge and put the container on the lowest shelf.

'A very special vaccine,' Simon replied, gently placing the second box on the work-top.

'So Mr Han said,' Anya remembered, 'but vaccine against what?'

'Leprosy.'

Anya's head snapped up. 'There isn't such a thing . . .' she began, then bit the words off. 'Sorry that was a dummb thing to say considering I've just handled it.'

'Dub, but understandable,' Simon grinned. 'It's so new these are the first human trials. That's why this trip is so special. We are part of the test programme taking place in several countries where leprosy is still a scourge. If the vaccine works it will become one of the miracles of modern medicine.' He disappeared again.

Anya began taking the tubes, boxes, jars and bottles out of the carton.

'Enter them on the stock sheet as you put them away,' Simon reminded her.

She nodded absently, studying the sheet, then she looked up frowning. 'Simon, everything is listed under it's chemical name, it was the same at the Pharmacy.'

'Of course, its less confusing——'

'No, that wasn't what I meant——'

'You want to know why the drugs aren't listed under brand names the way they were at your previous hospital, right?'

'Well—yes. You seem to have a very limited choice.' She scanned the shelves. 'Different formulations of the same drug can vary quite a lot in their effects so——'

'True.' He rested one hip against the corner of the cupboard and folded his arms. 'But perhaps you've forgotten that the F.C.S. was set up as a charity. Though we have a small grant from the Ministry of Health, every cent has to be accounted for. Of the thousands of drugs available only a fraction of that number are essential or genuinely useful.'

Anya opened her mouth to argue but his peremptory movement made her close it again.

'The British National Health Service allows free prescribing and the drugs bill is rocketing while hospitals are being closed through lack of money to staff and run them. Is that progress? The drug industry is exactly that, Anya, an industry, with profits to make and markets to find. They have a vested interest in promoting their products, regardless of whether they are strictly necessary. Considering our limited budget what am I to do? Do I allow my doctors to supply expensive brand-name drugs to a privileged few? Which patients should have preference? Children, because they are the coming generation? The middle-aged, because they are the wage-earners and have families dependent on them? Surely not the elderly, they may have worked all their lives, but their usefulness is almost over. Which would you choose, Anya?'

'That's not fair——'

'Life rarely is,' he said bluntly. 'What's fair about a world that spends more on arms in a single day than it would cost to feed all the starving for a year? What's fair about so-called civilised countries using valuable medical resources to treat self-inflicted illness, obesity, drug-abuse and alcoholism, while in the third world millions die simply for lack of clean water?' He straightened up. 'Our brief is to get basic medical care to as many as possible. Drugs have a vital role to play, but it is secondary to . . .' his gaze challenged her, 'you tell me.'

Anya's thoughts raced. How much she had taken for granted at Heathfield. So busy in her own department she had never looked beyond. Even after her decision to leave and her course at the School of Hygiene and Tropical Medicine, she had been so immersed in her studies there had been no time to stop and consider all the aspects and implications of medical care outside hospital. 'Er—pure drinking water, sewage disposal, education regarding diet and hygiene and' the corners of her mouth lifted in a wry smile, 'the encouragement of breast feeding.'

His eyes gleamed. 'I think you're getting the idea.'

Hoping he wouldn't notice her heightened colour and not even sure of the reason for it, Anya took refuge in briskness. 'But you do consider vaccines necessary?'

'Certainly,' he nodded, 'especially the B.C.G. Tuberculosis is rife out here, particularly among refugee squatters and the boat people. But we do have another string to our medical bow. Excuse me,' grasping Anya's shoulders, Simon squeezed past her and again she experienced a tightness in her throat and a weakness in her legs as his body brushed against hers.

He opened the double doors of the cupboard next to the refrigerator. A faint smell of herbs wafted on to the air. The shelves were crowded with glass and porcelain jars except for the top one and that held a number of bulging polythene bags.

'What—? It looks like leaves and twigs and lumps of root.' She turned her startled gaze to Simon.

'That's right,' he said simply. 'We aim to get the best of both worlds in the F.C.S. All these,' he raised his arm indicating the complete contents of the cupboard, 'are traditional Chinese remedies, tried and tested over centuries.' He lifted down a squat porcelain jar and removed the lid, holding the jar under Anya's nose. She sniffed cautiously. The greenish ointment had a faintly acrid smell but was not unpleasant. 'This is for boils, abscesses and other skin eruptions. It works in seventy per cent of cases. Where it doesn't, we use antibiotics.' He returned the jar to the shelf and pointed to another. 'This is Mongolian snake root, an excellent tranquilliser. There is aniseed, an appetite stimulant. I've used an injected infusion of sage for angina with marvellous results. We simmer bamboo leaves, mint, liquorice, berberous and chrysanthemum into a sort of tea which is an excellent tonic and preventive of upper respiratory tract infections.'

'What's that grey powder in the small bottle?' Anya was intrigued.

'Powdered spiders' skins.'

'You're joking,' she laughed, then added quickly, 'aren't you?'

He shook his head. 'It has a far quicker effect on certain fevers than anything modern science has to offer.' He closed the cupboard door. 'All this is bound to seem rather strange at first.'

'You can say that again,' she murmured, bemused. 'I'm still not sure——'

'Just keep an open mind,' he said. 'It's another possibility, another point of view. You might still conclude orthodox drugs are the best treatment in certain circumstances, but you'll have lost nothing and will probably have learned a great deal by considering alternatives.'

Anya made a face. 'I'll never be able to remember all——'

'I don't expect you to,' Simon cut in. 'I have some excellent reference books you can borrow. But don't imagine this is all there is to traditional Chinese medicine. We haven't touched on diagnosis. Give me your right hand.'

Anya hesitated.

'Come on.' He grew impatient.

Obediently Anya held out her hand and his fingers and thumbs closed gently on her wrist.

'Pulse taking is an art as much as a science.' His touch was light but his finger tips burned like a brand on the tender skin on the inside of her arm. 'It reveals not only the heart-rate through the number of beats per minute,' his voice was deep, hypnotic, running over her like dark honey, 'but also whether the beat is fast or slow, strong or weak, steady or irregular.' Unable to resist the impulse, Anya raised her eyes to his. 'And those in turn reveal a great deal.'

Aware that her body was betraying the tumult caused by his touch, and that he could clearly read what was happening, Anya tried to draw her hand away.

His hand closed around her wrist like a shackle and with a swift tug he pulled her close.

She gasped and tried to wrench free, but his other arm clamped around her waist holding her against him. His tautly muscled strength was like an electric shock. A fine trembling shook her, perspiration dewed her body and her heart thudded painfully against her ribs. What was happening? She had never felt remotely like this with Nigel. She barely knew Simon Brody, how *could* he affect her this way?

'Look at me,' he commanded softly. She shook her head quickly. Her throat was dry and she could not trust herself to speak. 'Look at me, Anya.' He did not raise his voice, but something in his tone brought her head up.

His gaze swept over her features coming to rest at last on her mouth. Sensing what was coming, knowing she was powerless to prevent it, Anya tried to turn her head.

'No,' he muttered. Letting go of her wrist he caught her chin between his thumb and forefinger, tilting it inexorably. Then his lips touched hers, soft as a breath, warm, coaxing, goading until her reluctant mouth began to respond.

But the instant her lips parted under his he released her, drawing his head back, studying her, his heavy-lidded eyes glittering like twin topazes.

Anya stared at him, her breathing quick and ragged. Without even realising it she clung to his arms for support, her legs like jelly as the floor seemed to rock beneath her feet.

'Of all the senses touch is the most powerful,' Simon murmured. 'Medical experiments——'

The word acted like a bucketful of icy water. Anya's eyes widened, and galvanised into action she tore herself free, her cheeks flaming as shame and anger welled up in her. Experiments?

What on earth had possessed her? Charles had warned her about Simon Brody and she had laughed, told him she was quite capable of taking care of herself. She was certainly off to a great start.

'Is that what this was all about?' She was furious as much with herself as with him. 'A medical experiment?'

Even now while she was literally shaking with anger she could still feel the gentle pressure of his lips. Part of her wanted to scrub at her mouth with her handkerchief, but deep down she knew that nothing would erase the memory of that kiss, a kiss more devastating than any she had ever experienced. Yet he was talking about experiments.

Simon frowned. 'Just a minute——' He took a step towards her, reaching out his hand.

She leapt back. 'Don't you touch me,' she warned.

They both jumped at the sudden rap on the open door. Susan Chang poked her head in. 'Excuse me, Doctors, coffee is ready.'

'Thank you, Susan,' Anya said quickly, and without a backward glance walked out of the dispensary.

## CHAPTER THREE

'DR Brody has just been telling me about the traditional remedies you sometimes use,' Anya said as she picked up her coffee.

Susan Chang nodded vigorously. 'Wherever possible he allows the patients to choose which they would prefer, Chinese or Western,' she beamed. 'This gives the patients more confidence in us, and we have fewer problems with acceptance and completion of treatment.'

Anya nodded and from the corner of her eye saw Simon emerge from the dispensary. She avoided looking at him and turned to Carol West. 'How about you, Nurse? I don't suppose it has much effect on your work in theatre?'

'Mmm?' The slender blonde started, her thoughts obviously elsewhere. 'Oh, not directly. We use conventional anaesthetics, and I.V. antibiotics where wound infection is a risk. But the patients are often more compliant, if an operation is required, than those I've seen in hospital who have been on a Western medicine only regime.'

'I think it's a matter of trust,' Susan added. 'Because we accept and use traditional medicine, they are prepared to accept ours. It's the best of both worlds,' she beamed again, echoing Simon, her eyes mere slits in her round, cheerful face.

'So I've been told,' Anya murmured. 'I'd better get back. Learning where everything is kept is one of the biggest problems in a new job.' She smiled at the nurses and, avoiding Simon's mocking gaze, returned to the dispensary still clutching her coffee.

Anger and confusion still warred within her. She needed to be alone for a while. But this was not the time to try and work out her personal problems. They would have to wait until tonight when she had completed her day's tasks and could relax in her cabin. Right now work was the best way to banish thoughts of Simon Brody. She had always been able to lose herself in her work, and all things considered it looked as though she would be relying very heavily on that ability during the weeks ahead.

Swallowing the last of her coffee Anya set the mug down near the back of the white formica work bench and resumed unpacking and putting away the rest of the drugs, concentrating on remembering the contents of each shelf in every cupboard. It was vital that, in an emergency, she should be able to put her hands immediately on whatever she needed.

Immersed in what she was doing, Anya was oblivious to time. Then a loud clatter made her jump. It came from the operating theatre and sounded as though someone had dropped a tray of instruments.

Was it her imagination or was the floor more unstable than it had been earlier? She tried to shrug the thought away, but the bottles on the shelves were beginning to clink together and when her coffee mug suddenly slithered off the work-top and shattered on the floor, she could no longer ignore the signs. The weather was worsening.

She heard the theatre doors swish and Simon Brody's quick footsteps, She was kneeling to pick up the pieces of broken china when his tall figure filled the doorway.

'What happened?' they asked each other simultaneously.

'Are you all right?' He frowned down at her.

'Yes,' she said quickly, 'the mug fell off, that's all. Was anyone hurt in theatre? I heard the crash.'

He reached into one of the cupboard drawers and took out some extra guard rails which he began bolting on to the open shelves, bracing himself against the increased pitching. 'Carol fell over a trolley. She wasn't hurt. Damn careless though.'

Reminded of the fair-haired nurse it occurred to Anya to ask Simon if he'd noticed her preoccupation and if so, had he any idea what was worrying her, as plainly something was. But his last remark pushed the thought aside. 'That's hardly fair,' she blurted without stopping to think, 'the weather is much worse.'

'The weather is fine,' he retorted, 'we're going through the Lyemun Pass. It's the currents that are causing the increased movement.'

Anya pressed her lips together. Increased movement? The boat was heaving and tossing like a cork. Suddenly it lurched violently over to one side and Anya lost her balance. She fell against the cupboard, landing on her bottom. Then the boat swung the other way, throwing her forward again. Her stomach churned, partly from fear and partly from another very unpleasant sensation she did not recognise.

Simon leaned over and, sliding a hand under her arm, hauled her to her feet. 'Get everything off the work benches, lamp, books, glassware, everything. Try and find space for it in the cupboards. Anything heavy must be as near floor level as possible.'

The noise from the clattering bottles grated on Anya's nerves as she tried to fit everything into the cupboards, but her hands were shaking and the heaving floor kept throwing her off balance. Perspiration broke out on her forehead and ran in cold trickles down her spine. She slid the cupboard door shut, then hanging on to the bench, hauled herself to her feet.

Simon was jamming paper towels between the larger bottles now held securely in place by the extra rails. He thrust a handful at her. 'You start at that end.'

Anya tried to steady her hands as she pushed the wadded paper into place. He must not see how frightened she was. He had warned her the conditions could be difficult and sometimes dangerous. But she had signed the contract and she was committed. Anyway, she tried to bolster her courage, according to him this wasn't rough, it was just 'more movement'.

Anya swallowed, trying to lubricate her parched throat. She sensed Simon's eyes on her and tried to assume an air of nonchalance.

'When we visit the Shatin Valley on one of our routine calls in a few weeks time,' he said calmly, 'I'll take you to Amah Rock.'

Anya doubted they would even reach this trip's destination. Clinging to the edge of the bench she moistened her lips. 'That sounds interesting.' Then realising she sounded totally uninterested, she forced the words out, 'What is Amah Rock?'

'A large lump of stone shaped like a woman carrying a baby. There's a rather beautiful legend attached to it.' His long legs were planted wide apart as he swayed, riding the boat's twisting leaps and plunges like a cowboy at a rodeo. 'A fisherman's wife with her baby strapped to her back in the traditional manner, used to go to that spot high on a hill overlooking the harbour to watch for her husband's return. But one day he didn't come back and she was told he had perished at sea. She refused to believe it and for a year she watched and waited. Then, so the legend goes, the gods took pity on her, and with a lightning bolt transported her and the child to her husband, leaving a stone monument to her fidelity.'

Anya looked at him. She was touched by the story, but even more surprised that he had told it to her.

'And not too far from there is a monastery, with a temple, a pagoda and several pavilions that contain ten thousand statues of Buddha. Of course you won't have seen anything of Victoria itself yet. The Thieves Market is a must. Rumour has it that anything stolen from you during the night will be on sale there the following morning. Though it's more likely the name is derived from the prices. Bargaining or haggling isn't only a general rule, it's an absolute necessity. Have you ever haggled?'

Anya shook her head, 'No, I've never been to the sort of places where——'

'You'll soon get the hang of it,' he broke in. 'Then there are the jade and ivory shops where you can watch the craftsmen working. A bridge carved from a whole tusk can take up to twenty days to make, depending on it's size and the intricacy of detail.'

'I . . . sh-shall enjoy the chance to explore.' She tried to smile, but gasped as the boat gave an enormous lurch. The floor fell away from beneath her feet, and losing her balance she grabbed at the bench and missed.

Simon scooped her up, holding her close with his arm around her waist. Forgetting the last time he had held her, forgetting how angry she was with him, how confused he made her, she clung to his shoulders, her eyes shut tight. Another lurch and the boat rolled so far sideways Anya was sure they were going to capsize. She tasted blood as her teeth bit through the soft inner side of her lip in her effort not to scream.

'It's rough here at the best of times,' he explained gently, 'because of the strong currents, but with a rising wind blowing against the tide it's worse than usual. We'll be through in a few minutes.' He was so calm, so matter-of-fact, she felt a pang of shame and it helped soothe her terror. His chin moved on her hair as he looked round. 'We've come through pretty well this time, no breakages—except your coffee mug.'

Even as he spoke the violent pitching seemed to ease. Anya hardly dared believe it, but as the seconds passed and the lurching lessened perceptibly, a tremulous sigh of relief escaped her.

Suddenly aware she was still clinging to Simon Brody, aware of his body heat, the pressure of his sinewy arms and the hard muscles of his thighs against hers, Anya drew away, her cheeks scarlet as she fumbled for words.

He caught her wrists. 'Anya,' he began in a low voice, but even as he said her name the thud of footsteps in the passage and the sound of the consulting room door bursting open jerked them both round. Giving her arms a brief but unmistakable squeeze, Simon released her and hurried out. Pressing her palms momentarily to her hot face, Anya went after him.

A short, plump Chinese wearing a white apron over his singlet and cotton trousers and a white cloth knotted loosely around his throat was holding the passage door open. As Anya entered the consulting room behind Simon one of the crewmen who had helped unload the taxi on their arrival, stumbled through the doorway, supporting his colleague who was groaning, barely conscious, one side of his face a gory mask and his once blue shirt splattered with crimson.

'Take him into theatre quickly,' Simon directed, then turned to the cook. 'Do you know what happened?'

The man was sweating profusely and kept dabbing his face with a corner of his neckcloth. 'Was accident, Dottah Blody. Some oil on galley floor, I spill when boat go——' he rocked his hands to and fro. 'I plan clean up very quick but pan on stove start to slide and I must catch, forget oil for minute. Kam-Li come to fetch coffee for Captain. Boat fall over again. Kam-Li step in oil, slip very fast and hit head on corner of table—very bad, very bad.' He dabbed his face again.

'Anya,' Simon was brisk, 'this is right up your street, you deal with it.' Without waiting for a reply he turned back to the cook and Anya, the adrenalin of fear now reinforced by the need for immediate action, fought the churning in her stomach and pushed open the theatre door. Behind her she heard Simon tell the cook to get the oil cleaned up at once, then the door swung shut.

Carol West tied the tapes on Anya's gown while she rinsed the hibitane solution off her hands and arms and dried them on a sterile towel. Susan and the other crewman had got Kam-Li on to the table and were fixing the guard rails so that he wouldn't roll off if the boat pitched or rolled suddenly.

For a moment Anya hesitated, completely still. She had never before worked under such conditions. The theatre seemed barely big enough for the table, the sink and the anaesthetic equipment. Yet there was also an instrument cabinet, the autoclave and a diagnostic trolley crammed in somehow. The nurses avoided each other with practised ease, Susan adjusting the overhead operating light while Carol's quiet voice penetrated the cotton wool that seemed to be fuzzing Anya's brain. 'Gloves, doctor?'

'Thank you.' Anya took a deep breath and, determinedly ignoring her discomfort, approached the table to begin her examination.

Simon entered quietly holding a casualty card and a pen. 'When you're ready, Dr Lucas, I'll note your observations.' Kam-Li was now officially her patient. Her eyes flickered briefly to Simon's face. His expression was bland yet for a fleeting instant she recognised in his amber eyes the light of challenge, not exactly hostile, but totally objective, demanding proof of her right to be there.

She turned her whole attention to Kam-Li. Completing her general examination, Anya asked for forceps and swabs and began to clean away the congealing blood with a mild antiseptic solution.

Having thoroughly cleaned the area Anya discarded the forceps and began feeling all around the edges of the ugly gash. Without X-ray or scanner, diagnostic aids she had used so often in the past, she had to rely solely on her own observations and sense of touch. There were no physical signs of brain damage, but a heavy fall against the stainless steel galley table could easily fracture a skull.

Perspiration formed in beads on Anya's forehead with the effort of bracing herself against the boat's movement while maintaining the light pressure.

Carol stepped forward and wiped moisture from the visible part of Anya's face with a swab, then withdrew again.

'As far as I can tell, there's no bone damage.' Anya wondered for a moment what they'd have done if there had been. Returned to Victoria to get Kam-Li to hospital? But what about all the other patients waiting for them? Thank God, she wasn't faced with that choice. 'However, the patient is likely to suffer moderate concussion.' She swabbed the wound once more then turned to Carol to ask for sutures.

When the jagged cut had been carefully stitched and a sterile dressing taped lightly over the wound, Anya checked Kam-Li's pulse and pupil reaction once more. 'He's stable,' she announced briefly, tugging her mask down over her chin. 'His colour is beginning to improve. He should regain full consciousness soon.'

'Do you want anything from the dispensary for him?' Simon asked as he put the top on his pen.

Anya shook her head and stripping off her gloves ran her fingers through her damp curls. 'Unless his headache is unbearable I'd rather not give him anything. It could mask any changes in his condition.'

'Right then, lunch.' Simon indicated the door as Anya shrugged off the gown. She turned to Carol who was starting to clear up. 'I've worked under easier conditions, but I can't say I've ever had a more helpful or efficient theatre team. Thank you both.'

A smile lit Carol's face banishing for a moment the tension around her eyes and the strain that tightened her mouth into a thin line. But even as Anya turned away the smile faded and the haunted expression returned.

'Call me if there's any——' Anya began, but Simon whispered to her.

'You've just praised their professionalism, let them get on with it. They *are* a good team. Carol will clear up while Susan watches Kam-Li, then they'll take turns to eat. They're used to this sort of thing.'

Anya glared at him, fiercely resenting his interference, after all the patient was her responsibility. Then, as quickly, her resentment died. He was right, they obviously knew what they were doing. She was the newcomer, the one who had so much to learn.

He pushed open the door holding it back for her to precede him. Now she was no longer engrossed, her discomfort had returned in force. Her stomach protested violently as the floor heaved under her feet. It was on the tip of her tongue to say that she didn't feel hungry, but she held the words back. It had been a hectic, exhausting morning. She glanced at her watch. It was almost two, six hours since her snatched breakfast. No wonder she felt low. A meal was bound to help.

'So, what do you think of the facilities?' Simon asked as they entered the saloon.

'They're—remarkable,' Anya replied. His dark brows lifted fractionally and she knew he was waiting for her to elaborate. She supposed she should express her admiration for the way all the essential equipment had been squeezed so functionally into the small space, but she felt too wretched. Was it the delayed effect of her long journey out to Hong Kong? Surely she wasn't going down with some bug?

The oblong table was set for four. Simon held her chair for her then seated himself opposite. The cook bustled in, placing a warmed plate in front of them both, then hurried away, returning moments later with a tray laden with bowls piled high with rice, stir-fried chicken, fish and a huge dish of red and green peppers, onions, peas and bamboo shoots.

Anya looked at the steaming food then reached for the jug and poured herself a glass of iced water. As she sipped it the Captain walked in. About fifty, he wore a short-sleeved blue shirt similar to Simon's and lightweight navy trousers. His short, black hair was covered by a dark blue peaked cap which he swept off the instant he saw Anya.

Simon made the introductions. 'Captain Ho, this is Dr Lucas.'

The Captain gave Anya a wide smile revealing a set of large, unnaturally even teeth in bright pink plastic gums. 'May I welcome you aboard, Dr Lucas,' he lisped, bowing across the table.

'Thank you, Captain. It's nice to be here.' Anya tried to return the smile, but her face was stiff and she knew her [illegible]npt was anything but convincing.

'Please don't allow me to interrupt your meal——'

'Will you join us?' Simon offered. The Captain shook his head.

'I have already eaten. But if I may have a moment.' His eyes flickered briefly towards Anya, then he looked squarely at Simon and made an almost imperceptible gesture with his head towards the door.

The beads of perspiration on Anya's forehead and upper lip owed nothing to fear. In fact the air-conditioned saloon was pleasantly cool, but she felt ghastly. If only Simon would go out as the Captain obviously wanted him to, she could push a little food about her plate, pretend she'd eaten, then escape to her cabin and lie down for ten minutes.

'Come on, Anya, don't let it get cold,' Simon said briskly. 'You know how important it is for a busy doctor to have regular meals.' He pushed the tray towards her. 'Of course I can spare a moment, Captain. Do sit down. You won't mind if I get on with my lunch? We're running a bit behind what with one thing and another.'

Anya felt a flush stain her cheeks as she remembered the scene, outside the Pharmacy. Plainly he intended to see she followed his orders this time. Wanting only to be ignored, Anya took small portions of rice, vegetables and chicken.

Simon asked about the latest weather report, but she barely heard the Captain's reply, such was the effort it cost her to swallow that first mouthful. Sweat trickled down between her breasts. For one terrible moment she thought she was going to be sick, but she sipped more iced water and after struggling through a couple more forkfuls, began to feel slightly better.

'. . . pressure falling fast,' the Captain was saying, 'even so I think we should use the channel between Joss House Bay and Lam Tong Island.'

Anya looked at Simon who was frowning and eating while he talked. 'That's a pretty rough passage with a south-easter blowing.'

The Captain spread his hands. 'Indeed, but a much briefer unpleasantness than if we go round the island first into the wind and then with it on our beam. There is also the time element.'

'OK,' Simon nodded, 'you're the expert. How long until——?'

Captain Ho glanced quickly at Anya then lowered his voice. 'Two hours at the most.'

Continuing to eat automatically, Anya kept her eyes lowered but now listened intently to the two men's conversation. It sounded as if something wasn't quite right. But what? She could hardly butt in to ask. Captain Ho could not completely hide his concern and would plainly have preferred to talk to Simon privately. If only she had listened more carefully at the beginning.

'Damn,' Simon grated under his breath. 'Where then?'

'North side of High Island. It's the best we can do in the time, and the cliffs live up to their name so we should have good protection,' Captain Ho replied.

'Fine. By the way Kam-Li has a nasty cut and probably concussion. Dr Lucas has patched him up but he'll be out of commission for at least thirty-six hours.'

'Thank you, Dr Lucas.' The Captain smiled politely. 'Forgive me for interrupting your meal.'

'Please,' Anya waved his apology aside and as he left she pushed her empty plate away. 'I'd better go and see how Kam-Li is. I expect the nurses will want some lunch.'

Simon touched her shoulder lightly. 'Kam-Li is in good hands and the cook will have taken trays down to

Carol and Susan. Do you want coffee?' She shook her head. The food lay in a solid lump in her stomach. 'Then come up on deck. The ride through the channel is an exhilarating experience and just around the headland is Clear-Water Bay. There's a big film studio complex there.'

How could she tell him all she wanted was to get off the boat on to firm ground or, failing that, to sleep away this awful queasiness? No special treatment, he had warned, and how definite she had been in not wanting any. She could just imagine the scorn that would curl his lip and harden those tawny eyes. Yet if she refused and didn't tell him she felt ill, he would assume she was rejecting his olive branch, and things between them were precarious enough already. She had no choice. 'Thanks, it sounds great.' She forced the words past a tight smile.

Simon led the way to the bow where they clung to the rail, the wind plastering their clothes against their bodies, flattening their hair and snatching both words and breath away.

Anya stared ahead at the channel between the peninsula and the rocky barren island. The sea seemed to boil as cross-currents and rip-tides resisted the pressure of water backed by the wind pouring through the narrow mouth of the strait. She gasped as the boat plunged and bucked, hurled like an eggshell first one way then the other. And as the Captain steered a course between the rocks that edged both islands and mainland like jagged black teeth, it seemed to Anya that one more gust, one more wave would surely drive the boat on to them.

Spray torn from the waves was dashed into her face and she tasted salt on her lips. She darted a look at Simon and blushed to find him watching her.

'Not quite as bad as the Lyemun Pass.' He grinned

and her colour deepened as she recalled clinging to him in her terror, and knew that he intended her to remember.

'I must be getting used to it,' she shouted back and realised suddenly that she wasn't afraid. Breathless, awestruck, excited, but without a trace of fear.

Then they were through the gap and after a couple of uncomfortable minutes as the boat turned broadside to the waves, the Captain brought her round and they were on the other side of the peninsula, surging forward, riding the waves like a giant porpoise.

'There are the studios,' Simon shouted above the roaring wind, pointing at several hangarlike buildings and a cluster of smaller ones.

'What kind of films do they make?'

'Spy sagas, adventure, pirates, war, comedy, romance. You name it, it's been filmed here. The British and Americans use the facilities as well.'

'There's not much happening today,' Anya yelled back.

'It's pretty quiet at this time of year. Imagine trying to cope with props, lights and microphones in this wind. Besides, the high humidity causing problems with the lenses.'

'What kind of problems?'

'A kind of fungus, due to condensation within the camera. It can grow overnight. We have the same trouble with microscopes and binoculars. In any case I expect they heard the warning.'

'What warning?' Anya asked. But he had turned away and was scanning the horizon.

'Come on, time to go.' He took her arm and Anya realised she had completely forgotten her discomfort. But though the air-conditioning was a blessed relief after the steamy heat outside, the moment they went below she began to feel queasy again. 'Will you excuse me a moment?' She drew away from him, one hand on the door of her cabin. 'I'd like to freshen up a bit.'

'Of course.' He was about to say something more, but changed his mind and with a nod moved on down the passage and disappeared into the consulting room.

After washing her face and hands and cleaning her teeth in the shower room, Anya felt a bit better. Back in the cabin she folded her towel over the rail on the side of the locker, and dropped her toilet bag on the top. While she was here she might as well unpack. It would only take a moment. Deep in her heart Anya knew that was only an excuse for remaining in the cabin a little while longer, away from Simon Brody.

It wasn't just that he was a big man, who seemed even bigger in the confined space of the boat, it was her own very mixed reactions to him. She wasn't even sure if she liked hom or not. She couldn't deny his attraction, but she had met attractive men before. Nigel had been considered quite handsome, yet neither he nor any of the other men she knew had ever affected her the way Simon Brody did. Perhaps it was those strange tiger-like eyes. Or maybe it was her. Perhaps she was still tired, or the heat and damp were getting to her. Whatever, her usual defences were letting her down. Sometimes she could swear he was reading her thoughts, yet there was about him a distance, a reserve she could not penetrate.

She rubbed her hands over the back of her neck and sighed, then straightened her back. Nor did she want to, she told herself firmly. None of this was important. A little awkward maybe, until she learned how to handle it, and be as casual as he, but not important.

She took her clothes out of the tote-bag and folded it up, laying it on the bottom shelf of the locker. Her toilet bag went on to the top shelf. It hadn't occurred to her to bring hangers. Still, maybe the wardrobe also had shelves in it. She pulled open the doors and froze. Oilskins, a bathrobe, jeans, shirts and underwear filled both hanging space and the shelves beneath on the right hand side. The left hand side was empty.

'Oh, no.' Anya felt her scalp tighten and goose-pimples broke out on her arms. She darted across to the other locker and wrenched it open. It was crammed full of books, a battery razor, a toilet bag and a rolled-up towel. She slammed the door shut and sat down suddenly on the nearest bunk, her head spinning. This was too much. Why hadn't he said anything?

The door opened and Simon's head appeared round it. One glance at the open wardrobe, Anya's pale angry face and set mouth brought him inside. He closed the door and leaned against it. 'I told you, yours is the other bunk,' he said, his face expressionless. 'I'm afraid two feet six inches just isn't wide enough for me.'

Anya leapt up as if she'd been stung. 'No way,' she snapped, her eyes blazing.

'Come on now, that's hardly fair . . .'

To Anya his reasoning tone was merely fuel to the flames of her anger. She was almost speechless. 'Hardly fair—? You have the nerve to talk about being fair?'

'Well, be honest, you're smaller and slimmer than me, you don't need a three-foot bunk.'

'For God's sake, I'm not talking about the bunks,' Anya shouted. 'Why didn't you tell me about this—this—arrangement? No, don't answer. It's perfectly obvious. I suppose you thought once we were at sea I'd be afraid to argue, well, you're wrong. You may be used to having your own way with everyone else, Dr Brody, but not with me. There is no way I'm going to share this cabin with you.'

'Really?' His voice had taken on a harder edge but he still appeared perfectly relaxed as he folded his arms. 'Then where do you intend to sleep?' He waited just long enough for her to open her mouth. 'Because there are only two sleeping cabins in the boat, apart from the crew's quarters; one for the nurses and one for the doctors. Each has two berths. A bunk each.' He stabbed his finger at them one after the other. 'I thought I had made it quite clear, you are not required to sleep with me.' Anya's cheeks flamed at the acid in his tone. 'I had hoped it would not be necessary for us to share the cabin, but circumstances have decreed otherwise.'

'What circumstances?' Anya demanded suspiciously, her mind whirling as she struggled to retain her anger, hanging on to it so as to keep other, more subtle emotions at bay. She had every right to be angry, she was totally justified. It was he who was in the wrong.

'Ones over which even I have no control.' His irony stung Anya's raw nerves like a lash. 'We're in the path of a typhoon. Had we reached our destination as planned, I would have spent the night ashore under canvas; as it is we'll have to seek shelter behind High Island for tonight, and hope we can go on in the morning.' He levered himself away from the door, resting his fingers on the handle. 'I warned you,' he said softly, 'difficult and sometimes dangerous, I said. No special treatment, no favours, remember?'

Anya looked at her hands, tightly clasped. She remembered only too well. She forced herself to meet his gaze. 'Yes.' Her throat was dry, the word barely audible.

Gone was the friendliness. His voice was cold, his expression forbidding. 'I've made all the concessions I intend to. I've explained things which should not have required explanations. You, Dr Lucas, signed a contract. I expect you to honour it.' His voice dripped scorn. 'There will be no more—scenes.' It was an order. 'Be in the consulting room in ten minutes.' He strode out and Anya, her legs refusing to support her any longer, sank down on to her bunk.

## CHAPTER FOUR

SOMEHOW Anya got through the rest of the afternoon. With the other crewman's help Kam-Li was taken back to his quarters. He had been sick but now felt much better apart from a dull headache. He tried to insist he was ready to go back to work but Anya firmly quashed the idea. Crossing her fingers behind her back she told him the Captain had ordered him to stay in bed until the following morning at least. Kam-Li didn't argue any further. The voice of authority, Anya thought wryly. She was the doctor, but it was what the Captain said that counted.

She prepared a list from the record cards of children in the settlement requiring routine vaccination against whooping cough, diphtheria, measles and T.B. She watched and listened as Simon described and prepared Chinese remedies for the ailments and infections he met on every trip. Then it was time for the evening meal.

There was an atmosphere of relief and good humour as the four of them sat down. It had been an exhausting day, but all the necessary work had been done despite their late start, Kam-Li's accident and the worsening weather.

Captain Ho put his head round the door to announce that they had reached their anchorage behind High Island and that the typhoon was likely to hit within the hour.

The cook brought in a large tureen of soup and set it on the table.

'This is shark's fin, Dr Lucas.' Susan beamed as she

poured two large ladlefuls into her bowl. 'It's really delicious. Here, you must try,' and before Anya could protest, Susan had ladled some into her bowl.

'That's enough,' Anya said sharply, adding a swift, 'thank you.' Then aware she had sounded abrupt, if not downright rude, she went on, 'Is it really made from shark's fins?'

Susan nodded and pushed the tureen towards Carol who also helped herself generously. 'Yes, they are simmered in chicken broth with cornflour, peanut oil and crab meat or perhaps a little sliced chicken.'

Anya fiddled with her spoon. The rich aroma of the soup made her stomach heave. Here we go again, she thought wearily and sipped some water. Alongside her, Simon was eating with obvious enjoyment. He was talking to Carol who, Anya noticed, seemed quite different. Gone was the abstracted air, the look of strain. Though she still appeared tired there was a suppressed, almost feverish gaiety about her as she responded to Simon's questions.

'So there are no problems with this extra duty?'

Carol glanced at him, wide-eyed. 'No, of course not. Why should there be?'

'Oh, I don't know,' Simon said, 'I was just thinking, domestic commitments, that sort of thing.'

Carol's face paled. 'What do you mean?' she said quickly, then laughed, a brittle sound, forced. 'Dr Brody, surely you haven't forgotten? I'm a single girl. No ties, no responsibilities, just what the agency wanted. This job and me, we're ideally suited.' Her archness jarred Anya's nerves, but Simon merely nodded.

Anya wondered what had wrought the change in Carol then, suddenly aware that Simon was watching her and determined to deny him any further opportunity for criticism, she concentrated on her meal, forcing the soup down her constricted throat, gritting her teeth as she made a show of enjoying it. Then it was finished and the cook cleared the dishes, basking in the compliments showered on him by Susan and echoed by everyone else. Next he brought in a vast mound of fried rice with pieces of egg, shrimps, ham, peas and green onions.

'Ah, Chow Fan,' Susan licked her lips. She obviously enjoyed her food and Anya envied her.

The meal seemed to drag on forever. It was clear that Simon used this opportunity at the end of the day when everyone could relax to sort out any problems that had cropped up, to rearrange timetables, switch duties and alter routines where necessary to the constantly changing demands on each member of the team. Once that was settled the conversation became general once more.

'Bill's hopeless,' Susan was saying. 'I wonder how Mary's coping with him. He never gets his requisitions in on time and it took me a week just to sort out the filing last time I was on his boat.'

'He'll have to get his act together soon,' Simon warned, 'or I'll replace him. Pam's got enough on her plate without having to chase round after him. He rang me the night before last, full of apologies . . .'

Feeling sick, bone-weary and out of place, Anya slipped out of her seat and quietly left the room. She couldn't face the tiny cabin, her mind shying away from the knowledge that in the next couple of hours she and Simon Brody would be preparing to spend the night together. When she had first seen the cabin it had struck her as small and at that time she had believed it would be hers alone. How on earth would they manage? This was one aspect of being the first woman doctor in the F.C.S. that had not occurred to her. She felt choked and claustrophobic. She needed space and room to breathe. She had to see the hills and the sky.

They were anchored in a deep narrow cove. Towering cliffs rose sheer on three sides and across the stretch of open water Anaya could discern the dark, rounded humps of the mainland hills. Stars twinkled, diamond-bright in the black velvet sky, as Anya stood in the stern. Outside the cove the wind had risen to a howl, lashing the water into spume-topped waves, but here, within the protective shelter of the cliffs, the air was almost still. Ripples slapped softly against the hull. She grasped one of the metal stanchions from which swung a dingy, and rested her hot forehead against her hands. A sigh shuddered through her.

'You haven't eaten a decent meal since we left Victoria,' Simon said quietly. Anya started violently, she hadn't heard him come up behind her. Letting go of the cool metal she moved away from him to the rail, her heart thumping unevenly. 'What's the matter?' His tone was a blend of irritation and concern.

'N-nothing,' she stammered. 'It's just the heat, and I haven't felt very hungry. I'm all right.'

'Claptrap,' was his succinct reply. 'I've been watching you. I want the truth.' He grasped her shoulder and pulled her gently, but firmly round to face him. 'What's wrong?'

She kept her eyes down. He saw too much, knew too much. This physical discomfort was nothing compared to the sudden loneliness that gripped her. She had always been so self-sufficient, capable, quite content with her own company, not missing Nigel at all when work or meetings kept them apart for days at a time, which should have told her something, she supposed.

Now, dramatically, when she already had so much to cope with, it was different. She wanted to lean on, to confide in, to draw from the vast strength of *this man*. The discovery, far from comforting, left her bereft and isolated. 'It's—it's just a slight stomach upset, not even that really. I'm fine up here on deck, or ashore——

Simon stared at her then gave a sudden shout of laughter that made her flinch. 'You idiot girl, you're seasick. Why in heaven's name didn't you say so?'

'Seasick?' Of course. She grimaced. 'I never thought, I mean I wasn't actually—I put it down to being tired or a bug of some sort. What a fool I am.' She gave a small self-mocking smile.

He laughed again. 'Seasick,' he repeated, shaking his head.

'I'm glad you find it amusing,' Anya was tart.

His grin faded. 'I wasn't . . ' He became impatient. 'Why didn't you tell me you were feeling ill?' He took her arm, 'Come on down to the dispensary. I've an excellent remedy that will have you feeling fine in less than an hour.'

'Lead me to it,' Anya said, the effort it had cost her to keep going showing in her voice.

'Why didn't you *say* something?' he repeated harshly.

She was too weary to dissemble. 'I thought you'd be angry. You'd see me as a liability, not pulling my weight, folding under the first sign of pressure or discomfort—besides, we'd already crossed swords a couple of times and I couldn't face——' She gasped as he stopped abruptly, jerking her round, his hands on her shoulders, pinning her against the wall of the narrow passage. There was a whiteness round his nostrils and the lines that bracketed his mouth were deeply scored. 'Do you really think I'm that much of a bastard?'

'Yes,' she blurted, then, 'no.' Anya shrugged helplessly. 'Oh, I don't know.'

Without another word Simon pushed her ahead of him into the dispensary. To her surprise he went directly to the Chinese medicine cupboard and took down a large bottle.

'What are they?' Anya stared suspiciously at the two dark brown tablets in her palm.

Simon thrust a small beaker of water into her hand. 'Papaya juice on a vegetable charcoal base. They're excellent for acute indigestion or intestinal irritation.'

'But if I'm seasick, what use . . .?'

He leaned against the bench and folded his arms. 'You haven't actually vomited, have you?' She shook her head. 'Then your balance mechanism isn't too badly affected. That will adjust on its own in a day or two. In the meantime all you need is something to settle your stomach.'

Anya was still reluctant. 'Don't you have any Dramamine?'

'Yes. But I'm not prepared to waste drugs on someone who doesn't need them.' Impatience roughened his voice. 'You know our system. Do you consider yourself superior to the rest of our patients?'

Anya was taken aback. 'What do you mean?'

'Herbs and such are all right for the peasants,' he was scathing, 'but not for you?'

'No, of course not——'

'Then swallow them. They work, I promise.' He grinned unexpectedly. 'We've all resorted to them at one time or another. The typhoon season is a testing time for even experienced sailors.'

Anya felt a great weight slip from her shoulders.

She wasn't the only one, the weak link in the chain. She swallowed the tablets. 'About all this,' she indicated the cupboard, 'do you have any books I could borrow?'

'Sure. They're in my . . .' he corrected himself gravely, 'in *our* cabin. Come on, I'll dig them out for you.'

Anya swallowed again, with more difficulty. One problem dealt with, another to be faced. What did she do now? A thought struck her. She hadn't packed a nightdress. What could she wear? Hysterical laughter bubbled inside her. What did it matter? She could go to bed in a mac and wellies if she chose, Simon Brody certainly didn't give a damn. He had made it crystal clear, they were only sharing the cabin, not a bed. But she wasn't used to sharing *anything*, not even her flat. She had never been that close to another person, male or female, had never wanted to be. She gritted her teeth. It wasn't her fault she was the first woman doctor in the F.C.S. which made the usual arrangements difficult. But nor was it Simon's fault a typhoon prevented him sleeping ashore. She would just have to get used to it. There was no alternative for either of them.

She followed him into the cabin and waited while he pulled two books out of his locker.

'This one is by Professor Hue-su Chang, one of the foremost authorities on traditional Chinese medicine.' He handed her a weighty tome. 'This other one is concerned more with tropical diseases and has an excellent chapter on leprosy.'

As she took the books, their fingers brushed and she felt warm colour rising like a tide up her neck and into her face.

'I'd get an early night if I were you,' he advised. 'I've got some paperwork to do in the office for an hour. That should give you time to . . .' He gestured vaguely and Anya suddenly saw that behind his calm, organised façade he was finding the situation as awkward as she did. Somehow that helped. Yet part of her wondered why a man of his reputation and experience should be embarrassed by circumstances which, while totally new to her, had to be quite unremarkable for him.

But for the air-conditioning the cabin would have been unbearable. As it was Anya threw off first her thin robe, then the blanket, pushing both to the bottom of the bunk. She lay propped up on two pillows, naked beneath the cotton sheet, cool and comfortable, making notes as she read.

Outside the wind screamed and howled and sudden squalls of rain hammered on the deck above her head and hissed into the water. But though the boat rocked, tugging at her anchor, Anya found the movement soothing and restful now that her stomach had settled. It was hard to keep her eyes open. The words on the page blurred, ran together . . .

A heavy thud woke her and she sat up, stretching sleepily, unable for a moment to remember where she was.

'Aphrodite rising from the waves,' Simon murmured and with a gasp Anya grabbed the sheet which had fallen to her hips and shot down the bed again.

Simon was sitting up in his bunk, a book in his hands and two more on his locker. The wall light attached to the bulkhead illuminated one side of his face and the bronzed skin of his arms and shoulders. Dark hair curled thickly on his chest extending down across his flat stomach to where the sheet covered him and Anya flushed deeply as she realised he was probably naked as well.

'It was your book,' he said.

'What?' Anya's thoughts were so tangled she didn't

grasp what he meant.

'Your book,' he pointed, 'it fell off, that's what woke you. You were asleep when I came in. I was going to prise it from your hands and put it on the locker, but had you woken to find me bent over you . . .' He let the words tail off and shrugged.

She'd have terrified the whole boat with her screams, that was what he was implying, Anya knew. But would she? In that languorous moment between sleeping and waking, her body warm and relaxed, would she have screamed and pushed him away? Or waking to his amber eyes, gleaming and heavy-lidded only inches from hers, would she have reached up to run her fingers through his dark mane, raking her nails lightly down his neck and across his massive shoulders as she offered him her lips?

Anya gulped and flushed scarlet. What was the matter with her? She had so readily accused him of trying to take advantage of her. She had been furious when he kissed her in the dispensary. But honesty forced her to admit it wasn't the kiss that had provoked her fierce indignation, it was that he should have used it as an experiment. The kiss itself had been—too tantalisingly brief.

'Shall I get it for you?' He leaned forward and one long brown foot snaked out from under the sheet towards the floor.

'No,' she cried instantly and quickly looked away from his mocking grin. Carefully, clutching the sheet around her, she leaned out of the bunk, picked up the text book and finding her jotter pad and pencil in the folds of her sheet she wriggled down to the bottom of the bunk and put them all on her locker. Then she lay down again, staring at the ceiling, burningly aware of Simon, lying in his bunk, so close, apparently engrossed in his reading.

She tried to empty her mind, to channel her chaotic

thoughts, to recall what she had just read, but it was useless. Scenes from the day flashed before her eyes like film clips; signing the contract in his study, his delighted smile when Ah Mai told him Kerry was calling from Switzerland, his terrifying rage outside the Pharmacy, his calm voice relating the legend of Amah Rock. So many facets. She understood now that his descriptions of places of interest they could visit were to take her mind off her fear. She hadn't realised before how many things she was afraid of. She had planned her life unconsciously avoiding involvement or commitment to anything but her job. Even her post at Heathfield had been chosen because while intellectually and technically satisfying, her contact with patients as people was minimal. They were usually 'emergency cases'. Many of the follow-ups, as they progressed and recovered and became people once more, were handled by other departments or her colleagues on alternate rotas.

But things were changing, more drastically than she had ever envisaged. The protective layers she had built up since her parents' death in a motorway accident as they returned home from a visit to the theatre to celebrate their eighteenth wedding anniversary, when she had been fifteen years old, were being peeled off like onion skins. Where would it end? Already she felt uncertain and vulnerable.

Mentally and emotionally drained, Anya turned on to her right side with a soft sigh. A sleepy smile curved her mouth at the sight of Simon's feet, half-uncovered, less than a yard from her face. She'd lie the other way round tomorrow. Her eyes fluttered closed, her lashes like fans on her flushed cheeks. She didn't hear the catch in Simon's breathing, nor did she see his book tilt sideways as he watched her, perplexed, a muscle jumping at the point of his jaw.

A vision of the bedroom she had occupied for that

one brief night at Simon's house drifted into her mind. It was so pretty, so feminine. Her breathing deepened but a tiny frown marred the smoothness of her forehead. With her last waking thought she wondered, who is Kerry?

The boat was under way again before breakfast. The increased pitching and rolling woke Anya from a dream-filled sleep. The wind had eased and rain no longer pounded the deck, though the sea still ran high. The cabin was empty and Simon's bunk was made. Quickly Anya slipped into her robe and clutching her toilet bag and towel, made for the shower. As she emerged she bumped into Simon coming out of the consulting room.

'Good morning,' he said gravely, 'I hope you slept well?'

'Yes, thank you,' Anya replied, her hand on the cabin door. 'And you?'

'Fine, thanks. See you at breakfast, I've got a couple more tablets for you.'

'Thank you,' Anya repeated and opened the door. They were being so formal and polite, no one would ever believe they had just spent the night together—well, she amended hastily, not *exactly* together——

'Anya . . .'

She turned and he lowered his head to say softly in her ear, 'You talk in your sleep.'

Anya went hot and cold. 'I didn't, did I?' she whispered, horrified, her mind racing, trying to recall her dreams, then trying to shut them out as she realised the subject of most of them was standing, all too real, right in front of her, *watching her face*.

'No,' he grinned, his eyes glinting, 'but I wish you had.'

'Oh,' she gasped, 'you——' She didn't know

whether to laugh or fume as he strode down the passage towards the saloon. Laughter won and as she dressed in the green cotton trousers and yellow T-shirt and tidied her end of the cabin there was a new lightness in her heart.

'We'll have to see how long it takes to clear the routine work before starting the leprosy tests,' Simon said as they arrived at the settlement. The Captain edged the boat gently alongside a crude breakwater that protected the small cove and its fishing boats. 'Anya, you go with Susan.'

'Go? Where?'

'Ashore,' he said crisply. 'We use the schoolroom as a baby clinic and for giving the routine vaccinations, which leaves facilities here free for whatever turns up.'

Anya glanced out of the porthole and saw a huddle of people, young and old, gossiping as they waited.

'Any other problems you refer to me,' Simon went on.

Anya stiffened. 'I assure you, I'm quite capable——'

'I don't doubt it,' he broke in, smothering a grin, 'but I don't think last night's study of Chinese medicine qualifies you to offer a choice of treatment just yet, do you?' She bit her lip and had to agree. 'Right then, let's make a start.'

Emerging on deck she was immediately dewed in perspiration, and her shirt and trousers clung damply. The gusting breeze was itself hot and heavy with moisture. Anya jumped on to the rough stones of the breakwater, staggering slightly as her legs tried to accustom themselves once more to solid ground. The black leather bag containing her equipment and the vials of serum bumped against her knee as she edged through the milling people, who stared at her in open curiosity.

Glancing over her shoulder she saw Susan carrying the white plastic box that contained sterile dishes, syringes, needles, antiseptic, cottonwool and dressings.

Behind her Simon appeared on deck, his bronzed skin even darker in comparison with his white short-sleeved shirt. He was talking to the waiting people and as he spoke they shuffled into an untidy line.

As they walked through the village Anya looked around her, struck by the air of timelessness and tranquillity. Life must have gone on in villages like these all over China, virtually unchanged for hundreds of years. She could smell woodsmoke and seaweed, fish and mud and frying onions. Above the stony beach where the undertow of breaking waves drew pebbles down into the water with a sucking hiss, several sampans lay safe above the highwater mark. Wooden posts were hammered into the turf and between them hung fishing nets, some simply drying in the sun, others being mended by weatherbeaten men and sinewy boys clad only in ragged shorts. Beside the boats was a pile of crab and lobster pots made of bamboo.

Chickens scratched in the short grass and bare earth and behind the nearer houses, built of mudbrick and roofed with bamboo and rice-straw, a flock of geese honked and preened beside a reed-edged pond. The rice crop, lush and green and almost ready for harvesting, rippled gently in the terraced paddies extending up the hillsides. Pigs snorted and squealed in a pen and a tethered water buffalo bellowed mournfully.

The schoolroom looked just like another house. The mothers were waiting, sitting on wooden benches while their children played and squabbled, their babble filling the air. There was a sudden silence as

Anya appeared and Susan introduced her. Anya felt horribly self-conscious as dozens of pairs of almond eyes swung in her direction and studied her from head to toe. She smiled tentatively and murmured greetings in Cantonese.

Whispers of surprise gave way to wide grins and nods and gradually the noise climbed to its former level. The smiles boosted Anya's morale though she was quite prepared to allow they could be amusement at her accent rather than genuine welcome.

After she and Susan had set out all the equipment on a wooden table covered with a green sheet, Anya called the children one at a time. With Susan acting as interpreter when necessary, she gave each a thorough examination ensuring there were no signs of illness or infection before administering the primary, secondary or booster injections. Though some children whimpered and shied away from the needle, Anya had no difficulty persuading them to swallow the sugar lump containing polio vaccine.

Two hours later they returned to the boat. Susan went into theatre to unpack and sterilise the needles and syringes. Anya went to the consulting room. 'We're finished ashore. Do you want any help?' she asked Simon as she opened her bag on the examination table and took out the unused serum.

He looked up from the treatment card he was completing. 'How did it go?'

'One six-month-old boy has a middle-ear infection and I saw an eighteen-month-old girl with eczema on her legs. I've asked the mothers to bring them down here. Three due for booster shots didn't turn up, but apart from those we completed the list.'

'Good.' He stood up and hefted his bag on to the desk, quickly checking its contents. 'There is something you can do, see to the last patient. His name is Kim-wan, he's fifteen and has an infected hand, looks like an abscess. Carol's cleaning him up now. He'll need antibiotics.'

'I daresay I can manage that,' Anya said crisply.

Simon looked up quickly. 'Now what's all that about?'

'I'm not a first-year student.' The words came out in a burst of irritation. 'I have held a responsible position for quite some time.'

Unexpectedly he grinned. 'Sorry, force of habit, I have to specify for the nurses. I'm not used to working with another doctor, especially one——' He broke off. 'Was there something else?'

'Yes,' Anya retorted, her feathers still ruffled, and wondering what he had intended to say before obviously thinking better of it. 'Where are you going?'

'A house call. While you're in the dispensary can you get me twenty morphine sulphate tablets from the narcotics cupboard?' He passed her the key.

'Terminal?'

He nodded. 'All I can do is ease the pain.'

Anya's irritation dissolved immediately. She could hear frustration and helplessness in his voice, though he was fighting to control both. She made no reply. What was there to say? She knew what he was feeling. With all their knowledge and training, with all the technological advances and wonder drugs, there were still some patients for whom they could do nothing except relieve pain and allow death to come peacefully and with dignity. Perhaps there was a lesson there somewhere.

Putting the unused serum in the fridge, Anya collected the antibiotics then unlocked the dangerous drugs cupboard. She had to throw up her hand to stop the boxes and bottles tumbling out on to her.

Quickly pushing everything back on to the shelves she swiftly sorted the different narcotics into their correct order. Taking a flat-packed white cardboard box from the drawer, she slotted it into shape and counted the twenty film-coated brown tablets into it. About to relock the door she hesitated, frowning. She ran her eyes carefully over the lower shelf once more, then locked the cupboard and returned to the consulting room. Simon was just coming out of theatre.

'Got them? Thanks.' He dropped the box into his bag, the scuffed black leather betraying many years of travelling and service, and snapped it shut. 'As soon as you've finished get some lunch, and if those mothers arrive before I get back, you see to the children, I leave the treatment to your discretion.' He made for the door.

Something was bothering Anya. 'Simon, the C.D. cupboard looked as if a bomb had hit it.' She fingered the key.

'Probably the rough passage through the Lyemun Pass or behind Lam Tong Island.' He was dismissive.

'It's not just that,' Anya said awkwardly. 'I think something's missing.'

'How could it be? Nobody's been in that cupboard since we left Victoria.'

'I have, when I was unpacking the Pharmacy order. I put away fifteen ampules of diamorphine powder. That's three boxes.'

'So?'

'Well, there were two boxes when I started. Those plus the three I unpacked made five. There are only four now.' As Anya was speaking, Carol put her head round the theatre door.

'Anya,' Simon sounded impatient, 'there's no way five ampules of diamorphine could just disappear. You must have made a mistake either at the Pharmacy or when you were unpacking. Failing that you've put the box back on the wrong shelf. Did you check the stock list against the order sheet?'

'Not just now, no. I hardly had time——' Anya protested.

'Then perhaps it might be an idea to do so, *after* you've seen your patient. Did you want me, Carol?'

The nurse shook her head quickly. 'No, I wondered if Dr Lucas——'

'She's just coming.' His tall figure vanished along the passage.

Anya pushed the key into her trouser pocket and took the antibiotics through to theatre. After greeting the boy and reassuring him in halting Cantonese, she turned to Carol. 'Have you taken his temperature?'

The nurse nodded. 'It's slightly up.'

Anya looked closely at the boy's hand. It was angry-red and puffy. The abscess itself, between the thumb and first finger on the back of Kim-Wan's left hand, was a taut mound an inch across with a yellow head on it. A red streak was beginning to run towards his wrist. 'We've got this just in time,' Anya said quietly. 'What work do you do? Your job?' She asked Kim-Wan as she checked his pulse.

'I'm a fisherman, with my father.' His forehead was furrowed with pain.

'Carol, I'll want lignocaine spray, scalpel, swabs, gauze, saline and a sterile dressing.' The nurse began preparing a tray and Anya scrubbed her hands. 'Do you know how this happened? When it started?' She said over her shoulder.

Kim-Wan shrugged, holding his hand tenderly against his chest.

'Four, five days.' He went on in a torrent of words,

few of which Anya caught. She looked helplessly at Carol.

'I think he nicked it with his knife when he was gutting fish,' the nurse explained. 'It was only a very small cut.'

But the knife had been slippery with fish offal, blood and scales, more than enough, especially in this climate, to set up a core of infection which was beginning to leak into the boy's bloodstream.

Anya explained to Kim-Wan what she was going to do, looking to Carol for help when her vocabulary proved inadequate. The boy nodded and sat on the chair, resting his arm on the towels spread over the table. Carol stationed herself in front of Kim-Wan as she held his hand steady, so that he would not see and be upset by the unpleasant but necessary procedure.

Working swiftly Anya sprayed lignocaine over the whole hand to numb it. Pulling on disposable gloves she swabbed the hand once more, then with one quick incision she opened the abscess. Infected pus spurted out and in it Anya saw a dark speck. It was a fish scale.

Another few minutes saw the abscess drained, irrigated with saline, the cavity packed with gauze, then a sterile dressing bandaged over the wound.

'That's it.' Anya stripped off her gloves. 'Now I have to give you an injection to stop the infection spreading.'

'But no hurt now, all better——' Kim-Wan started to get up. Anya pushed him down again.

'Carol, explain will you? He must come back to have the dressing changed tomorrow. Also he ought to rest the hand for a couple of days.'

'No fishing?' The boy looked worried.

Anya shook her head. 'Not for two days. You must not get that hand wet or dirty——'

'But I must work,' Kim-Wan insisted. 'No good lie at home, lose face.' He winced as Anya withdrew the needle and rubbed his shoulder with spirit-soaked cottonwool.

Anya wished Simon were there. What should she do? 'Face' was very important in Chinese culture, perhaps even more so to these villagers who had very little else. 'Listen,' she said, 'most of the poison has gone, but there might still be a little bit in your hand which will grow and give you a lot of pain unless you do as I tell you, O.K.?'

'O.K.' The boy grinned, his black hair flopping over one eye.

'Carol, can you bring me a pair of disposable gloves, largest size.' Anya turned back to Kim-Wan. 'You must keep you hand clean and dry.' She took the polythene gloves from the nurse. 'Thanks. Now, when you are in the boat or you are handling fish or nets, put one of these on. Understand?' The boy nodded. 'Before you sleep tonight, take one of these capsules and another in the morning as soon as you wake, before you eat anything.' She handed him the gloves and the box. 'And for the next few days drink lots of water, at least ten cupfuls every day. It will help flush the infection out of your system.'

Kim-Wan grinned shyly. 'I go now?'

Anya nodded. 'Mind you're back here tomorrow afternoon to have that dressing changed.' She walked with him to the stern, making him repeat her instructions, then watched him trot over the breakwater, the rough stones making no impression on his leathery soles. He disappeared up the track to the village.

Turning to go below Anya reached for her hanky to wipe her forehead and throat, and her fingers touched the key. She hesitated. Should she check the cupboard now? Simon had been so sure it was simply a careless mistake on her part. Perhaps it was. Maybe the fright and the warning he had given her outside the Pharmacy had caused her to over-react. But it wasn't aspirin they were talking about, it was diamorphine—heroin. She dropped the key into her pocket once more. Nothing would be required from that cupboard for the rest of the day and she had the only key. She'd check again tonight when she had more time.

The nurses had eaten and gone and Anya was lingering over a cup of coffee when Simon returned. 'How is he?' she asked. He shook his head briefly.

'How long?'

'A week, a month, who can tell? But he's peaceful and the family are coping well. I said I'd look in again tomorrow, but I get the impression they'd just as soon I didn't.'

'How ungrateful,' Anya was cross. 'You've done all you can——'

'Exactly,' Simon interrupted. 'They know that, so from their point of view there is no point in my intruding on what is a private family occasion and they're quite right. It's my sense of helplessness that makes me want to go back, my need to reassure myself there was nothing more I could have done.' His gaze was level and candid and Anya knew as he turned away and sat down to the plate of food the cook had brought in, that Simon Brody was not the man of steel his demeanour so often suggested. Nor did he consider it a blow to his professional pride to lose a patient. The old Chinese peasant had been more than just a patient to Simon. He had cared for him as a person.

Anya said nothing, but shyly rested her hand, just for a moment, on his shoulder as she left the saloon, instinct telling her he wanted a few minutes alone.

She had never felt involvement with any of her patients. Her emotions had always been kept tightly under lock and key. She had justified her distance and reserve by reminding herself that women's emotions ran nearer the surface then men's and if she allowed hers to spill over on to her work she would not be able to function as dispassionately and objectively as her job demanded. How could she possibly evaluate the condition of an accident victim, assess damage, initiate life-saving procedures, make instant decisions when faced with set-backs and complications, if she was agonising over the pain the victim was in or the terrible grief and shock their family was suffering? It wasn't possible. Was it? For the first time in her career Anya wondered.

Twenty minutes later Simon opened the bottom drawer of his desk, took out a large, thick envelope and shook out the photographs it contained. 'Take a look at these and tell me what you see.'

Anya picked up the coloured photographs one at a time, examining them carefully. Simon adjusted the desk lamp, looking over her shoulder. She was aware of his closeness, his warm breath on her neck. She concentrated hard. 'They are all of Chinese children, between the ages of about five and fifteen.' She studied the photographs closely, re-examining several she had put aside. 'They all seem to have a similar skin lesion, a small patch slightly lighter or darker than the surrounding tissue, with an ill-defined edge.' She glanced at him. 'Is this it? Leprosy?'

He nodded. 'There is usually some nerve involvement, loss of sensation.'

Anya rifled through the photos. 'I always imagined it looked far worse. I remember reading dreadful, heart-rending accounts of leper colonies in Africa and on MoloKai in the Hawaiian Islands.'

'Before the development of modern drug treatments, the mutilating effects of the disease were horrific, but not any more.' His arm rested lightly against hers. 'If treatment is started within two years of the initial symptoms appearing there's almost one hundred per cent possibility of total cure. One of the sad things is that in three-quarters of all children presenting with skin symptoms, the lesion will disappear without treatment.'

'Sad?' Anya was puzzled. 'Why sad?'

'Because we daren't wait to see which way it will go. We have to begin treatment to minimise the risk of others being infected, and there is still an ancestral fear and social stigma attached to this disease.'

She looked up at him, her expression rapt. 'What a breakthrough it will mean if this new vaccine works.'

'That's the crux of the matter,' Simon warned. '*If* it works. I told you yesterday, we're one of several groups in different countries taking part in a double-blind trial. Some villagers will receive the vaccine, others won't.'

Anya rubbed her arms. 'That's one aspect of drug trials that always bothers me. If you discover something which will prevent or cure a disease, how can you justify using it only on certain people when others who need it just as desperately are denied?'

'You know the reasons,' Simon reproved, gently. 'We need scientific and unbiased proof, not only that it works, but that there are no dangerous side-effects. A properly conducted trial comparing two groups both exposed to or suffering from the disease, with only one receiving the new medication, is the only way.'

Anya turned back to the desk, leafing through the photographs once more. 'I know you're right,' she admitted, 'it's just . . .' She slid the photographs back into the envelope. 'How long before we know if the vaccine is effective?'

'Ten years,' came the blunt reply, 'and at least ten thousand people will have to be vaccinated for the statistics to prove anything. Meanwhile we continue the trials, plus treating any already infected as well as running our routine clinics. So for the next few months you are going to be busier than you thought.'

'Great,' Anya smiled. 'I haven't exactly been stretched these last couple of days. I know you were letting me settle in, and my stomach was doing its best to reverse the process,' she pulled a wry face, 'but I'm fine now and it will be marvellous having a real challenge.' It will leave me less time to think, to dream wild, stupid dreams, Anya thought, fiddling with a corner of the envelope.

Simon raised her chin with his forefinger, regarding her with a frown of puzzlement. 'You continually amaze me,' he murmured, and under his scrutiny she blushed deep rose.

'Why, because I'm a doctor who likes hard work?' she countered, striving for lightness while her heart performed a slow somersault.

'My experience of female doctors is very limited, so I'm in no position to compare.' His fingers traced the line of her jaw to her ear then slid lightly down her neck to rest on her shoulder. Anya tried to suppress a shiver of delight. 'About women, however, I know quite a lot,' he paused. Kerry, she thought. 'Or, I thought I did. Until now.' There was a moment's silence then he squeezed her arm. 'Come on, there's someone I want you to meet.'

He would say nothing more and they left the boat and made their way in the stifling afternoon heat towards a crude wooden hut set back from the pond and slightly apart from the cluster of houses that made up the settlement. Sweat trickled down Anya's back, soaking into her shirt. Her hair clung in damp tendrils to her neck and forehead. The breeze was an oven blast and the sun hammered on her skull. Smells she hadn't noticed that morning assailed her nostrils; rotting fish, the sickly sweet scent of decaying vegetation, stagnant water. Fat, black flies buzzed about her head and she swatted at them uselessly.

Beside her, Simon raised his arm in greeting. 'Madame,' he called, 'are you receiving guests today?'

Startled, Anya looked first at Simon, then at the figure clad in black tunic and trousers, struggling with the aid of a stick off a stool beside the door of the hut.

The woman had silver-white hair which straggled over her shoulders, surprising Anya who had not seen one woman outside Victoria with her hair down.

'Dr Brody, this is indeed a pleasure.' The woman's voice was low and clear and suddenly Anya realised with a shock that both Simon and the woman had spoken in English.

They covered the last few yards to the door of the hut where the woman waited, motionless. Simon grasped her upper arms and kissed her wrinkled, brown cheek, then he stepped back and Anya felt her smile of greeting freeze as she caught sight of the woman's hands and feet.

## CHAPTER FIVE

IT took all of Anya's willpower and training to calmly meet the old woman's steady gaze, to raise her eyes, without flinching, from the deformed, truncated limbs. She cleared her throat. 'I—I'm Dr Lucas.'

'Anya is my new assistant,' Simon added, then turning to Anya said, 'This is Madam Sen, a very dear friend and a courageous lady.'

The old woman had not taken her eyes from Anya's and Anya was startled to read compassion in them. 'As you see, it is not possible for me to shake hands in the Western manner,' she tucked the fingerless stumps into her sleeves and bowed, 'but I welcome you to my home.' Though her voice was quite high-pitched, her English was fluent and accent-free and her manner so gracious that for a moment Anya quite forgot Madam Sen's home was a crude hut on the edge of a small, isolated fishing settlement. She glanced quickly at Simon, waiting for him to speak, wondering why he had brought her there. But his face was expressionless.

Why didn't he say something? Give her a clue, a lead? Then she realised, this was a test. And with realisation came the instictive certainty that the whole course of their relationship depended on the next few minutes, on how she handled herself and the situation.

Sensing that the old lady's exquisite manners would not permit her to sit unless her guests were seated, and having no chairs to offer them, Anya folded her legs and dropped cross-legged on to the grass. 'Forgive me, but I'm not used to this heat. I came out from

England only a few days ago.'

Madam Sen smiled and inclined her head, then eased herself down on to the stool, waving aside Simon's helping hand with a gesture so unconsciously imperious that Anya bit her lip to stifle a grin. Her back was ramrod straight and Anya knew it was not shame or embarrassment that caused the old lady to draw her scarred toe-less feet out of sight, it was courtesy, so that her guests should not be disturbed by an offensive sight. And it *had* been a shock, Anya couldn't deny it. She received an even greater one a moment later.

'Ah, England,' Madam Sen smiled fondly. 'Such a pretty little country, so many trees. Even the cities have trees, in the gardens, along the avenues. I so admired the London Parks. During the Japanese occupation of Hong Kong all the trees were cut down and burned for firewood. The island is only just beginning to recover from that wanton destruction.'

'You've been to London?' Anya couldn't hide her surprise.

Madam Sen nodded. 'Twenty-nine years ago. I was twelve years old.' She saw the impact her words had on Anya. 'Yes, Dr Lucas, I am forty-one years old, and I look at least sixty. But I am alive. Leprosy did not kill me as it did so many others.'

'When did you contract the disease?' Anya asked. Fascinated by the extraordinary woman, she had completely forgotten Simon, who lay sprawled on the grass beside her.

'I was eight when the first patch appeared on my right knee. I came from a wealthy and powerful family, Dr Lucas. My parents took me to many doctors, refusing to accept the diagnoses. No child of theirs could be a leper, it was just not possible, the doctors had to be wrong. But clutching at straws, they tried every remedy traditional medicine offered. There weren't many. The worst was *fai chong chee*. It had an utterly revolting taste, a nauseating smell and no effect at all. Then they took me to London, to every specialist they could find. But still the diagnosis was the same. I saw them change.' She paused for a moment, a faraway look in her eyes as she relived the experience.

'You will not understand what a crushing blow this was to them, Dr Lucas. I was their only child, it was not possible for my mother to have more. In China all parents long for sons. Sons are their investment in the future, a continuation of the family line, a blessing from the gods. Girls are of so little importance that until recently many families killed them at birth.' Anya gasped. 'It is a custom that goes back thousands of years. So you see, for my parents it was disaster. First, that their only child should be a girl, and then for her to contract leprosy, a disease shrouded in fear and suspicion. It was too much.'

Despite the heat, Anya shivered. 'What did they do?'

'They took me to a leper colony in the Western New Territories and left me in the care of a relative of one of our servants.'

'They just abandoned you?'

'They had no choice,' Madam Sen replied gently. 'My father's business would have suffered. The family would have lost face. My mother would no longer have been received by relatives or friends. I was a leper, unclean, so therefore my parents were tainted, too.'

'But you could have been treated.'

'That was irrelevant, don't you see? I had *caught* the disease.'

'But how did they expain your absence?'

'To them I was dead. They burned all my clothes and toys, and said prayers for me. All the ceremonies were observed. Their child no longer existed. All this was explained in a letter entrusted to the woman who was to look after me. She died three years after I went to her. That was when I saw the letter. I was almost sixteen, alone, without protection. The people in the settlement,' she paused delicately, 'did not observe conventional rules of behaviour. I ran away and began the journey that finally brought me here.'

'But how did you survive? What did you live on?' Anya was totally engrossed in the woman's tragic story, unaware of Simon's gaze fixed on her face, his amber eyes hooded, watchful, revealing nothing of the thoughts behind them.

'I earned money while I could, writing letters for those who had not learned how. My tutor had always praised my calligraphy.' Involuntarily Anya's eyes dropped to the shapeless lumps of flesh half concealed by the baggy sleeves. But there was no self-pity in Madam Sen's voice, she was simply stating facts. 'When I could no longer work, I begged.' She paused. 'There are many kind people in the world. I reached this place six years ago. I was going blind and thought I would die here. But God is good.' For the first time she looked away from Anya and rested her gaze on Simon.

'Dr Brody was visiting and found me. He gave me medicine which healed my scars and averted the blindness. The disease was controlled and finally cured. But best of all he did not try to send me to another leper colony. He made a bargain with the villagers that I should earn my food by looking after the ducks and geese. I know them all, I have given them names.' Her face glowed with gratitude. 'He helped build this hut, my first home in twenty-five years.'

Simon, who had begun fidgeting, sprang to his feet. 'Enough,' he said curtly. 'What little I've done has been a privilege.' He leaned down and kissed the wrinkled cheek, murmuring softly, 'You are a very special lady.' Anya, while agreeing wholeheartedly, was startled by the pang of envy that knifed through her.

Simon grasped her arm and helped her up, the action unthinking, automatic, as he continued talking to Madame Sen. 'Is there anything you need?'

She shook her head. 'I have food, shelter. What more could I ask?'

'And the villagers?' Anya asked as she brushed dust and dry grass from her trousers, 'Do they help you? Do you have people to talk to?'

'They have accepted me,' Madam Sen answered carefully. 'Our lives have been so different, we have little in common but survival. Perhaps that is the greatest bond for all mankind.' She bowed her head gravely. 'I have enjoyed your visit, Dr Lucas. I trust you will find great satisfaction in your work, though no doubt much is still strange.'

Anya's grin was wry. 'Indeed, it is.'

'Goodbye, Dr Brody. Thank you for coming.'

It was uncanny, Anya thought, almost as if they had been granted an audience which was now over. Impulsively she turned. 'May I come and see you again, Madam Sen? I know so little of Hong Kong and its people, you could be of such help.'

The shabby, white-haired woman inclined her head regally. 'I should be delighted.'

Anya waited until they were half-way down the track and out of earshot. Then the words spilled out. 'I had no idea how much people like Madam Sen must have suffered. I don't mean the physical effects of the disease, though those are bad enough, but the rejection. Family, friends, even strangers turning their back, terrified of the slightest contact. Madam Sen was an innocent victim, yet she was treated like—like a loathsome criminal.' The force of Anya's feelings showed in her voice. Then came bewilderment. 'I've never talked to anyone like Madam Sen before. In Casualty I always concentrated on the damaged body. There was rarely time to consider the emotional aspects of the situation, and anyway,' she hesitated, 'I didn't think they were my concern.'

Simon looked down at her. 'And now you do?'

She shrugged helplessly. 'I—I'm not sure. Madam Sen—with her it's impossible to separate the two. I can't think of her simply in terms of her deformed hands and feet. She's a person, an indomitable lady who happens to lack fingers and toes because of disease. The emphasis is entirely different,' her voice dropped, 'and much more demanding.'

'Caring about people usually is,' Simon said coolly. 'It requires courage and emotional stamina. If you are going to be any real use as a doctor, you *have* to care. Weren't you ever taught that negative emotions, like fear, loneliness, grief and anger can predispose towards or even result in illness? There's been enough research done on it. The reverse is just as true, genuine caring and affection for our patients *as people* is as important a weapon in our fight against disease as the drugs we use.'

Do I have that kind of courage? Anya wondered as they boarded the boat. She thought of Madam Sen. Despite the terrible things that had happened to her, she had displayed not a single hint of bitterness or self-pity. In fact, Anya had sensed sympathy for *her*, as if the Chinese woman recognised her difficulties in coming to terms with all she was learning.

When Anya returned from the shower and slid gratefully between the cool sheets, she picked up the text book Simon had loaned her and opened it once more at the chapter on leprosy. She wanted to be certain exactly what to look for when they began the examinations the following morning.

She was deep in concentrated study when Simon entered the cabin. Anya glanced up. He was wearing the blue bathrobe she had seen in the wardrobe. It barely reached his knees and judging from the hair that curled darkly on his chest, he wore nothing under it. 'Do you want anything before I get into bed,' he asked. 'Books? Notepad? Glass of water?'

She shook her head. 'No, thank you.' Her eyes flickered to the porthole. The black sky was cloudless and brilliant with stars. The breeze had dropped to a whisper. The forecast for the night was good, and as Anya met Simon's steady gaze she read his challenge. There was no reason why he should not sleep ashore, under canvas, as he had originally intended. His eyes showed he knew it and knew that she did, too. He was waiting. Anya knew if she referred to it, he would keep his word and leave and she would have the cabin to herself. It was up to her. She felt her body grow warm and her cheeks begin to flush. She should speak, send him out, deny the attraction he held for her. To remain silent was foolish, worse, it was dangerous. Silence would slide her into uncharted waters, into a situation where she was no longer in sole control. But words would not come.

He leaned over and pressed the light switch above his bunk. 'Damn,' he muttered as the bulb remained obstinately dark. He pressed the button again.

'Perhaps the bulb's gone,' Anya suggested.

'Well, I'm not going in search of one now.' Simon grinned. 'I'll just have to share yours.'

Anya's eyes widened. 'What do you mean?'

He pulled out the sheet where it was tucked into the bottom of his bunk and transferred his pillow from the other end. As he loosened the tie-belt, Anya looked quickly down at her book, her face burning.

The robe thumped softly on to the floor, the bunk creaked and the sheets whispered as Simon climbed in. He adjusted the pillow behind his head, his black hair, damp and tousled from the shower, less than a foot from her face.

'God, it's good to lie down,' he yawned.

Anya smiled. She had felt exactly like that. But she dared not look up, nor did she trust her voice. Simon heaved a comfortable sigh then picked up his book and began to read.

After twenty minutes during which she had not absorbed a single sentence, Anya decided to admit defeat. Whether she was tired or it was Simon's proximity that was wrecking her concentration, it was obvious she wasn't going to learn anymore that night. Putting the book down on the floor, she turned her pillow over to find a cool place and settled down, her eyelids heavy. She yawned. ''Night, Simon,' she said without thinking as her eyes closed.

She vaguely heard him move, and the thump of his own book hitting the floor. Then the light clicked off and the cabin was dark.

'Good night, Anya,' his voice was soft, the words a murmur deep in his throat. Somewhere in the distance she heard him turn over. His fingers touched her hand as it lay palm-up, fingers loosely curled, beside her head. Then his lips brushed her forehead, her cheek, her nose. Startled, she turned her head, but before she could utter a sound, his mouth came down warm, gentle and tasting faintly of mint toothpaste, on hers. Her breath caught and for an instant she froze. She had lived this moment in her dreams. Was she dreaming now, or was this real? The kiss deepened and her lips parted beneath his tender assault. Simon's fingers closed convulsively on hers while his other hand traced the curve of her cheek, the line of her throat, her bare shoulder, and pushing aside the thin sheet strayed over the soft swell of her breast.

Anya's eyes flew open and she stiffened, clutching his shoulder, making a tiny gasping sound. Her heart was pounding and blood roared in her ears. Heat flooded her body, as every nerve vibrated. Nothing had prepared her for this. She was drowning in a whirlpool of sensation. 'No,' she groaned against his mouth, pushing him away with all her strength.

He tore his lips from hers with a suddenness that made her cry out. In the darkness she could see only the deeper blackness of his silhouette. His breathing was harsh, ragged and she knew he was fighting for control as he eased himself down into his bunk. The trembling that racked her gradually ceased and with it went her fear. She felt empty, oddly bereft, then she realised their fingers were still entwined. She wanted to explain, to make him understand. 'Simon——' she whispered tentatively.

He lay on his own pillow, his head turned away from her. 'Go to sleep,' came the brusque reply. But he didn't let go of her hand.

It was a turquoise and pearl morning as they made their way over the breakwater towards the village. The wind had dropped completely and there was an almost unearthly stillness in the air. Sounds from the stirring village carried clearly with the fragrance of wood-smoke.

As the sun, a shimmering gold disc, ascended the eastern horizon tinting the faint streaks of cloud rose-pink, the temperature was already beginning to climb. The pastel shades of dawn were crushed beneath the metallic brightness of another tropical day.

'Won't we be needing the nurses?' Anya asked as they walked up the track to the centre of the village.

Simon shook his head. 'Carol is doing antibiotic injections, dressing changes and urine tests and Susan is in the galley brewing up a couple of gallons of herb tonic.'

Anya tried to hide her smile but wasn't quick enough.

'Oh ye of little faith,' Simon snorted. Neither by word or sign had he referred to the previous night, yet strangely Anya felt no awkwardness. Alone in the cabin while she dressed, Anya had wondered if Simon knew he was the first man to rouse her to such intoxicating heights of sensuality. She was twenty-seven years old. There had been other boyfriends, but though their company had been enjoyable and their kisses pleasant, none of them had stirred her body, her mind or her heart the way Simon Brody did. Did he know that? Did she want him to know?

Their eyes had met over breakfast and his expression had been quizzical and oddly pensive. Had last night lowered his guard too? A new link existed now, a bridge that could join or separate them. Would she have the courage to cross it next time? She wrenched her attention back to the present and Simon's retort. 'I'm sorry, but you have to admit it does sound odd.'

'So did the idea of antibiotics being developed from mouldy bread,' he interrupted. 'Those herbs contain vital elements and minerals in their natural form. They are an excellent tonic and prevent coughs, colds and bronchitis. I could give the villagers synthetic pills containing the same chemical formula, but they would cost a hell of a lot more. Where is the medical or economic sense in that?'

Anya had to admit he was right and pulled a wry face.

'Don't worry,' he grinned, 'you'll get used to it.'

'I suppose so. We're dishing out a witch's brew on one hand and testing medical science's latest vaccine on the other, that's quite a contrast.'

Simon called greetings to the villagers, reminding them they would be called later, as they bustled in and out of their houses, feeding the livestock, fetching water from the single tap on the main street, shaking out the stiff quilts that served as both mattress and cover on their beds.

Children followed them, curiosity dancing in their almond eyes. The older boys who would shortly be helping in the rice fields or vegetable patches, or on the fishing boats, wore singlets and ragged shorts, while the youngsters, chattering like shrill magpies, scampered about in baggy pyjama-like suits of beige or black cotton. They reminded Anya of dolls with their round flat faces and straight black hair.

'Where does the vaccine come from?' she asked. 'I thought it was almost impossible to culture leprosy bacteria.'

'It was, until someone discovered that armadillos suffered from the disease. Then the researchers had a readily available source of bacteria and were able to develop the vaccine from there.'

'Just how bad is the problem?' Anya instinctively lowered her voice.

'In the colony generally it used to be very bad, with something like thirty people in every thousand showing signs of the disease. But since the Ministry set up primary health care teams specialising in the identification and treatment of leprosy, that number has fallen dramatically.'

'What about the people who had it before the teams were set up? What's happened to them?'

'There are special hospitals, which undertake reconstructive surgery and rehabilitation. The Chief Surgeon in Hong Kong is an incredible woman. She's done some truly amazing work and given hundreds of leprosy victims a new lease of life, not to mention restoring their confidence and pride in themselves.'

'Hundreds? That's marvellous, but——'

'There are still thousands like Madam Sen, I know,' he said shortly. 'I offered her the chance, but she refused. Her life has changed too drastically. She likes it here, she's at peace with herself and her surroundings.'

'Does anyone else here have the disease?'

Simon shook his head. 'The team came through two years ago and pronounced it clear. One of the reasons these outlying villages were chosen for the trials is that the populations are small, usually static and have little contact with the cities where T.B. can be an added complication.' He was studying her intently.

'What's the matter,' she raised one had uncertainly, 'have I got dirt on my face?'

'Morning light in the tropics is cruel to white women, but you—you remind me of a peeled lychee.' Anya's eyes widened. 'Cool and fresh with a delicate fragrance and a taste that is indefinable but very, very addictive.'

She bit her lip as a tide of dusky rose climbed her throat and flooded her face.

'We'll bring the table outside on to the schoolroom veranda and screen it. One of the village elders can send people through.' Simon continued making arrangements while Anya tried to concentrate, but she felt light-headed with happiness.

'It's far better to do the examinations in a good

natural light,' he explained, 'the skin changes are so subtle they're easy to miss. You might come across impetigo, scabies and patchy eczema. Ringworm and psoriasis can also be confused with leprosy lesions. If you're in any doubt, refer them to me.'

'You mean I'm to do examinations on my own?'

'Of course,' he said crisply. 'I don't carry passengers, remember? There are over a hundred people in this village and it would take far too long to do the lot by myself. If you're satisfied there are no signs of the disease, give the injection.' He opened the insulated box, revealing a top tray containing two separate sets of vials.

'Why are they marked A and B?'

'One set contains the vaccine, the other a salt water solution.'

'But which is which?'

'I haven't a clue,' he replied. 'I told you, it's a double-blind trial. Only the manufacturers know. That way there can be no bias in treating the patients, or cheating with the results. So choose, A or B?'

'I'll take A.' Anya set out the bottle of antiseptic, cotton wool, and dishes for the syringes, while Simon checked a list of the villagers names and sent two small boys to fetch their families. 'What's the distribution pattern?' she asked.

'In adults it's more prevalent in men, but in children it occurs equally in both sexes.'

They began work at opposite ends of the veranda, separated by a woven bamboo screen which provided privacy as Anya examined the women and girls and Simon checked the boys and men.

The villagers filed through one after another, coming singly and in families, from the fields, their homes and their boats, returning the moment their names were crossed off the list.

By midday Anya had vaccinated twenty-four women and children and referred five questionable skin lesions to Simon. Susan arrived with their lunch of cold chicken, fruit and coffee. While they ate she reported the morning's work.

'Kim-Wan has been in to have his dressing changed. He says he knows it's early, but the boat is going out this afternoon and won't be back until very late.'

Anya nodded. 'How is his hand?'

'Carol says it's healing well. She's reduced the gauze packing and the inflammation has almost gone. He had kept the bandage dry and clean and asked for another pair of disposable gloves.'

Anya grinned. 'That young man will go far. Did you give them to him?' Susan nodded.

'Urine tests complete? Ante-natals all O.K.?' Simon chipped in as he got up off the step.

'Yes, Dr Brody.'

Anya downed the last of her coffee and scrambled to her feet, dusting off the seat of her trousers. She was about to join Simon who was washing his hands in preparation for the afternoon's work, when Susan touched her arm. 'Dr Lucas, I—it's——' Her worried expression surprised Anya who couldn't remember seeing her without a beaming smile.

'What's the matter, Susan?'

The nurse twisted her hands together. 'It may be nothing—I—Kam-Li came into the theatre just before I left. He said he wanted to thank you for what you did yesterday. Then he offered to help bring the jugs of herb tonic up to the village this afternoon when it's cooled, but . . .' She hesitated then it came out in a rush, 'I think something is wrong.'

'Wrong? In what way?' Anya glanced across at Simon who was unpacking fresh syringes.

'The way he was walking, he was being so careful,

and touching things.' Her round face was clouded with concern as she looked up at Anya. 'I don't think he can see properly.'

'Did you say anything about it to him?' Anya asked quietly.

Susan shook her head. 'He made it clear he wished to speak to you, so I pretended not to notice. I did not want to alarm him. It is difficult you see—I—I mean we——' She lowered her eyes and her olive skin glowed pink.

So that's how things are, Anya thought. She patted Susan's shoulder. 'I understand. I hope you persuaded him to go back to bed?'

'Oh, yes,' Susan nodded quickly. 'I said you would be most angry if you returned to find him wandering about when he should be resting, in fact you would probably tell the captain.' She looked up pleadingly, 'I hope you didn't mind, Dr Lucas, but——'

'No, that's all right,' Anya's smile was wry. 'The main thing is to keep him lying still. Keep the cabin dim and try to persuade him to sleep. I'll come and see him as soon as I get back on board.'

'Thank you.' Susan's gratitude made it clear that Kam-Li was more than just a friend.

'What was all that about?' Simon demanded as Anya swiftly washed her hands. While she explained he lifted a fresh tray of vials out of the container. 'I've promised to see him as soon as we're finished here.'

'Damn and blast,' Simon swore with suppressed violence.

'What is it?'

'This tray of vials is damaged. Vaccine has leaked into the bottom of the container. How the hell can that have happened?' He carefully eased each vial out of the tray, inspecting it carefully. 'Check your batch.'

Anya did so. 'These are all O.K. How many——?'

'The whole row on this side,' he growled. 'The amount was carefully calculated, which means we are not going to be able to finish this village without replacements. Hell.' He hit the table with his fist, making the dishes rattle. 'Look, remove six from your batch and we'll press on until we've both used exactly the same number of doses.'

It was late afternoon when Simon called through the bamboo partition, 'I've run out of vaccine, how are you doing?'

Anya struggled to keep her voice level. 'Come through a moment, will you?'

The round, doll-like face of the little Chinese girl was serious as she looked up at Anya who held the child's left arm.

To Anya's relief Simon did not ask any questions except the child's name. 'Pik-Sen Lin,' Anya said quietly, 'according to the list she's six.'

'Hello, Pixie.' Simon knelt down in front of the little girl and began chatting to her in Cantonese. Only when a smile widened the little rosebud mouth and she turned her head away shyly, peeping sideways at him, did Simon gently take her arm and examine the ring-shaped brownish patch about two centimetres wide, while Anya watched, praying she was wrong.

'I'll hold her attention, you test for loss of sensitivity,' he directed and patiently coaxed the little girl to follow his pointing finger and tell him who lived in the houses, and what the animals were called, while Anya pricked the patch with a pin, then drew a feather over it. The child never flinched, she did not even glance at her arm, and Anya felt a sinking sensation in the pit of her stomach.

'No reaction,' she reported softly.

While the child giggled at something Simon had said, covering her mouth with her hand, he turned to

Anya. 'Have you ever done a slit-smear test?' She shook her head. 'Then this will be your first. There's a scalpel and slides in my bag. I'll keep Pixie occupied.'

Anya hesitated, 'Simon, perhaps——'

'Do it,' he grated, his eyes flint-hard.

Pixie's mother watched in silence as Anya took the sample. Suspicion was beginning to crease her forehead. As Anya swabbed the incision and covered it with an adhesive plaster, Simon prepared an injection. As he approached with the syringe, the mother's face cleared. Her child was after all having exactly the same treatment as the others.

'What is that?' Anya muttered.

'Lepromin skin test,' Simon answered. 'Just pray we get a positive reaction.'

Anya looked startled for an instant, then remembered, positive would mean it wasn't the more dangerous multibacillary type.

Simon administered the injection, then after making Pixie laugh once more, sent the little girl and her mother on their way.

'How long do we have to wait?'

'If there's going to be a reaction, it will show in a few days.'

'But aren't you going to say anything to Pixie's mother?'

'Not until I'm absolutely sure. The signs are pretty conclusive, but I want to be certain what type of leprosy she has. If it's tuberculoid, Pixie could be completely cured without any residual effects in eighteen months, but if it turns out to be lepromatous, the whole business will take much longer.'

'How much longer?' Anya forced herself to ask, thinking of the trusting little face framed by stiff black hair.

'Ten years at least. In either case the situation will need careful handling.'

'They're bound to be upset,' Anya admitted. 'But she *can* be cured. The treatment is quite simple, dapsone tablets twice a week——'

'You're not dealing with sophisticated people,' Simon interrupted. 'There's still a terrible stigma attached to leprosy and without very careful counselling the parents might simply leave the village, go somewhere else where they aren't known and begin a new life.'

'But without treatment——'

'I know. Pixie would get worse. She would also spread the disease wherever they went, *if* they took her with them.' Anya was horrified as the full import of his words sank in. 'But that's not all that worries me. Pixie's parents were among the few who did not want Madam Sen to stay here. I explained to them and to the rest of the villagers that she no longer carried the disease, that no one else could catch it from her. But how do you think they'll react now? And who will they blame? I need time to work out the best way of handling it.'

The light was mellow and hazy as a huge red sun sank towards the purple hills casting long shadows. Anya followed Simon across the breakwater. A trace of breeze, like gossamer on her skin, was just enough to stir the hot, moist air, but not sufficient to cool, or to dry the perspiration that soaked her shirt. He helped her on to the boat. 'Give me your bag. You'd better go and see Kam-Li straight away while I prepare the slide for examination.'

Anya nodded, trying to shrug off the depression that bore down on her like a heavy weight. Pixie was young, she was well nourished. Leprosy *could* be completely cured. But superimposed over her mental picture of the little girl's smiling face was that of a forty-one-year-old woman, white-haired and deeply lined, with no fingers or toes.

Anya walked quickly down the passage. What was the matter with her? Where was her detachment, her objectivity? Pixie and Madam Sen were patients, like hundreds of others she had seen. Only they weren't the same. Nothing was the same, because she was beginning to care. They mattered to her, not just as patients but as people. How was she going to cope with that? Oh, Simon Brody, she cried silently, what have you done to me?

Kam-Li was lying, eyes closed, on his bunk. But the moment she entered the cabin Anya knew he had not slept. He radiated fear, though he responded politely to her greeting and immediately tried to get up.

'No,' Anya pushed him gently but firmly back. 'Stay where you are. I want to examine your eyes and it's much easier if you are lying down.'

'My eyes? Why?' The question came too quickly.

'Because it's quite common after a severe blow to the head for the sight to be mildly affected.' She was matter-of-fact. 'Look at the light and try not to blink.' She leaned forward, examining Kam-Li's left eye with her ophthalmoscope.

'Such effects are not—permanent?' He was so deliberately casual Anya knew at once Susan had been right.

'Good heavens, no.' She turned his head to examine his right eye. 'I expect you've found things a bit fuzzy?'

'Yes.'

'More than a bit?'

'Yes.'

'One eye or both?'

'The right one.'

Anya moved the ophthalmoscope a fraction and found what she had suspected. 'You have a partially detached retina.' She sat up, switching off the instrument as Kam-Li blinked rapidly.

'What is that? What does it mean?'

'The eye is like a hollow ball and the retina is the inner layer. The bang on your head caused part of the retina to come loose, like paper peeling off a wall, and some fluid has got behind it, distorting your vision.'

'Will it go back on it's own?'

'It could,' Anya nodded, 'but it might take some time. It would be far better for you to go into hospital where the repair can be done quickly. You'll be back at work much sooner.'

'Really?' Kam-Li's relief was so patent, Anya had difficulty hiding her smile.

'Really.'

His delight quickly faded. 'But the Captain—and Dr Brody—if I cannot work—there is so much to do——'

Anya shook her head. 'Don't worry. We have to return to Victoria tonight in any case, to pick up more vaccine. You'll be transferred straight to hospital, and you should be back on board with both eyes working properly in time for the next trip.'

Kam-Li's grin threatened to split his face. 'Thank you, Dr Lucas, thank you very much.'

Anya got up. 'Just stay there and rest, the less you move the better. I'll send Nurse Chang along with the tray.'

He looked startled. 'Nurse——? But the cook . . .'

'I'm the doctor, and I think Nurse Chang, don't you?'

'Oh, yes pl—, as you say, Dr Lucas.' Kam-Li's

face was scarlet.

Smiling to herself, Anya closed the door and went back down the passage. After reassuring a worried Susan Chang and sending her to fetch the invalid's supper, Anya went through to the dispensary. The boat vibrated as the engines roared into life. She heard the anchor chains clanking and moments later the boat began to move.

Simon was hunched over the microscope, adjusting the eyepieces. Anya waited, surprised to find herself holding her breath.

He looked up and grinned. 'No bacilli. It looks as though it's tuberculoid. The skin test should confirm it.'

Relief made Anya's knees weak and she returned Simon's grin. Why should it matter so much? What were these people to her?

'Go and get your supper,' he directed, 'I'll put this lot away and I'll be along.'

'Shall I give you a hand?' she offered at once, but wasn't too disappointed when he shook his head.

'No, I'll only be a moment. Give me my key., will you?'

Anya pulled it out of her pocket and handed it over.

'Tell the cook I'll be right there. You can bring me up to date on Kam-Li while we eat.'

Anya nodded and left. Should she mention the budding romance between the crewman and Susan Chang? There was no reason not to, but what if relationships between medical staff and boatcrew were frowned upon? She might cause problems. Besides Simon might wonder at her motives and her own feelings were anything but clear right now.

After their meal, Anya returned to the cabin to pack. Simon had told her it would take at least twenty-four hours to obtain the replacement vaccine, so they would not be on board again until Sunday morning. As she looked round the tiny space, Anya felt a pang of regret, which she immediately quashed.

Simon poked his head around the door. 'Leave that and come up on deck.' He didn't wait for her reply. Anya dropped her toilet bag on the bunk and went after him.

Darkness provided a perfect backdrop for the multi-coloured lights of Victoria and Kowloon ahead of them on either side of the strait, and for the cluster of lanterns and lamps bobbing on the water a hundred yards away. 'What is that?' Anya rested her arms on the rail, pointing through the gap in what looked like a seawall at the lights.

'Causeway Bay Typhoon Shelter,' Simon replied. 'It's a floating village really.'

Now Anya could see that each lantern was fixed to a mast. The larger junks had several. All the boats were tied up in neat lines. Canvas awnings stretched over wooden frames protected the occupants from sun and rain, and were festooned with washing, ropes, sacks, buckets and boxes.

'How on earth do they manage?' Anya wondered. 'I mean what about shopping and——'

'All their needs are supplied by other boats,' Simon explained. 'Groceries, fresh fruit and vegetables, fuel, even flowers are ferried up and down the lines by enterprising sampan-owners.'

'But surely the authorities should be doing something about housing for these people?'

Simon leaned on the rail beside her. His arm touched her shoulder and she absorbed the warm contact like a sponge. 'Hong Kong has a population of over five million, most of them refugees from Communist China, living in an area of roughly ten square miles. Except they aren't evenly spread out but concentrated on the coast. You see those huge blocks of flats behind the shelter?' He pointed. 'They are part of a government housing project. Each block holds approximately thirty thousand people, that's over one hundred thousand residents on each estate. The government has provided schools, banks, markets and clinics.' He paused, turning to face her, leaning on one elbow. 'Imagine living in one of those blocks. Families are crammed in like sardines. Mothers have to carry their babies on their backs, there's no room for a pram. The most popular form of transport in Hong Kong is the bicycle, but people in those flats have no room to store one, so either they hire or walk. Laundry is dried on a bamboo pole stuck out of the window, or hung off the balcony which itself is used to store things there's no room for inside. Playing space for children is so limited that the flat roofs are fenced and turned into nursery schools and recreation areas. There is constant coming and going and noise.

'Many of the boat people have been offered flats but choose to stay where they are, cramped, but mobile. Most earn a living from fishing or supplying other boats. The larger junks act as lighters, shifting cargoes from coasters to the warehouses. If someone rows with a neighbour they can tie up alongside someone else. They have a choice, and they own the few square feet in which they live. Which would you choose?'

Anya looked at the avenues of boats, the lantern glow revealing families huddled under their canvas shelters around glowing charcoal stoves, eating, gossiping and laughing. The stark poverty of their surroundings and lack of privacy was mocked by the security of tradition and continuity. She looked beyond to the massive concrete towers, at the washing hanging like pathetic flags in the light of naked bulbs and imagined a seething ant-heap. She threw Simon a wry glance. 'I take your point.'

They passed the typhoon shelter and ahead of them a neon rainbow of shocking pink, lime green, electric blue and lurid orange lit the sky. The scent of exhaust fumes, flowers, drains and hot, spicy food wafted over the rippling water. The sounds of people and traffic, of juke boxes and radios blaring out twanging Chinese music and the thumping rhythm of Western pop songs carried over the waves from the gaudy strip.

'Where's that?' Anya asked.

'Wanchai. Where all the visiting servicemen go for—entertainment, a sort of oriental Soho.' He pushed himself upright. 'We'd better collect our gear.' He started below. 'Oh, I meant to tell you, I checked the C.D. cupboard myself. There's nothing missing.'

'What?' Anya stumbled after him.

'I said nothing is missing. The stock list, the order book and the boxes of diamorphine ampoules all tally. You made a mistake.'

'But I didn't, I'm positive——' She broke off. She couldn't understand it. When she had opened the cupboard and had to tidy the shelves there had been only four boxes of diamorphine, she'd have staked her life on it. Now Simon was saying there were five. So where had the other one been? How had it suddenly reappeared?

Thrusting her belongings into her tote-bag, Anya tried to shrug off her unease. After all, it was ultimately Simon's responsibility, and he was satisfied that everything was correct. Why should she worry?

Simon unlocked the front door and as they walked into the house Anya had the oddest feeling. She had come home. It was even stronger when, after dropping his briefcase in the study, Simon went towards the kitchen. 'You get the first shower,' he called over his shoulder, 'I'll make us a drink. What would you like, tea, coffee, or fruit juice?'

'Oh, I'd love a cup of tea,' Anya said gratefully and started up the stairs.

She had unpacked and, fresh from the shower, was sitting at the dressing table in her thin robe, combing her damp curls when, after a brief knock, Simon walked in with a tray. On it was a cup of tea, a plate of biscuits and a slender vase containing some sprigs of jasmine whose sweet fragrance immediately filled the room.

'Oh, how lovely,' Anya exclaimed, leaning forward to inhale the perfume as Simon rested the tray on a corner of the dressing table. She glanced up to see him watching her and his expression brought hot colour to her cheeks.

Unaccountably nervous she stood up, tightening her belt, playing with the comb, unable to meet his penetrating gaze.

'As we're going to be stuck in the city for twenty-four hours, I'll show you around,' he said quietly.

'I'd like that.' She smiled her thanks, and their eyes met.

'We'll make an early start.' His glance flickered over her.

Anya held her breath. Would he kiss her? Did she want him to, because if he did——. Involuntarily she swayed fractionally towards him. He took half a step forward then abruptly turned away, reaching for the door handle.

'Simon . . .' His name slipped out, she had no idea what to say next.

His jaw tightened, she could see a muscle working at one side of it.

'I'm going up to the hospital for an hour.'

'To see Kam-Li? Can I come with you?

He shook his head. 'There's no problem. I simply want to make him understand about post-op bed-rest. Four weeks is a long time and it will only hinder his recovery if he's fretting about loss of face, or being replaced.'

Anya looked down. The rebuff, though gentle, was firm.

'You'd better get some sleep,' he was curt. 'Good night.'

'Good night,' she replied bewildered.

Lying between the cool sheets she closed her eyes, but sleep would not come. After tossing and turning for a while Anya got up and went to the window. Drawing back the curtains she looked out on to the moon-silvered garden, its timeless serenity a soothing contrast to the conflict raging inside her. Two nights ago she had been furious when Simon insisted they share the cabin. Tonight she had space and privacy in a pretty room, which for the moment, she could call her own.

Yet she yearned to be back in the bunk at right angles to Simon's, his tousled black hair just touching her pillow, the sheet tangled around his bronzed, naked body. She turned restlessly from the window. She had to stop these thoughts, get things into perspective.

She and Simon had been thrown together in an intimate situation. He had kissed her. So what? People kissed all the time, it didn't necessarily mean anything. He was a very attractive man, no doubt he had had, maybe still did have, a fleet of girlfriends.

Anya held her breath against the knifing pain. She had no right to be jealous. One kiss wasn't a declaration, it offered no commitment. It might have transported *her* into realms hitherto undreamed of, but he had broken away, had refused to talk. Why should he, she tried to reason with herself. Why should she imagine because *she* was falling in love, that he—she froze, then gripped the windowsill with both hands, her knuckles white.

She couldn't be falling in love with him. The idea was ridiculous. They had only known each other four days. But, she reminded herself, during those four days, they had spent almost all their waking moments in each other's company, in an incredible variety of situations. They had seen more of each other, in every sense, than she and Nigel had in the three months before she left Heathfield.

Part of her wanted to rejoice, to laugh and revel in the glory of her discovery, but the other half was terrified. She was more vulnerable now than she had ever been. She risked rejection and a hurt such as she had never known.

And what of him? What did he feel? He was so self-contained. She knew he cared deeply about his work and his patients, but about her? She couldn't be sure. They were getting on well professionally, and he found her attractive enough to want to kiss her, but . . .

The moon's icy radiance bathed Anya's face but the peace and beauty of the night were lost on her as she struggled to come to terms with the revelation which, for better or worse, had changed her life forever.

# CHAPTER SIX

'ARE you sure you're all right?' It was the second time in fifteen minutes that he'd asked her. She had to pull herself together. Anya swallowed the last of her breakfast coffee. 'I'm fine,' she managed a smile. 'I had a bit of a restless night, that's all. The floor and the bed were much too still.' Realising what she'd said and the interpretation he could put on it, she blushed and turned away, carrying her cup and plate to the draining board.

Simon joined her at the sink, piling his own dishes on top of hers. 'I know what you mean. That cabin is so small, even after all this time I find it takes me a night or two to adjust to space and solid ground. Still, considering the lack of room on board, I guess I've been lucky. You're a very economical person.'

'I'm what?' Anya glanced round at him. What did he mean?

'You don't thrash about in your sleep and you don't scatter your belongings about all over the place. Most of the women I know appear to observe a rule which requires them to stake out their territory by spreading clothes, shoes, make-up, and bottles of perfume over as wide an area as possible.' He gazed into her eyes. Anya's heart turned over. 'You're not like that.' He sounded surprised.

She said nothing. His observation indicated that not only had he been watching her more closely than she realised, but also as she was the first woman doctor employed by the F.C.S., and therefore the first to sleep on a boat, his other experiences had most likely taken place in this house. She recalled the pretty bedroom she was using. The furniture, the colours, so obviously a woman's choice. Kerry. She had phoned him from Switzerland. How long would she be away? Was it work, or was she on holiday? That Simon would accept a reverse charge call from her with such pleasure signified closeness, a bond beyond mere friendship. Who was Kerry? How much did she mean to Simon?

Needing to do something, to blot out questions to which she had no answers, Anya turned on the hot water and put the dishes into the bowl.

'Leave those.' He was abrupt. 'Ah Mai will be in soon and she'll be cross if she thinks you're trying to take over her job.'

'I wasn't,' Anya protested at once. 'I didn't mean——'

'I know you didn't. But we've got so little time, I don't want to waste any. Are you ready?'

'I won't be a minute.' Anya raced upstairs, cleaned her teeth and hurried into her bedroom to apply a touch of lipstick. She flicked a comb through her cinnamon curls, and a last glance in the mirror reassured her that her trousers and overblouse of tan glazed cotton looked crisp and cool. Slinging the strap of her bag over her shoulder she hurried down again. So little time. What did he mean?

Simon was waiting for her in the hall. His eyes brightened as she reached his side. Once again he seemed to divine her thoughts. 'This time tomorrow we'll be on our way back to the settlement so let's make the most of today.' He broke off and in a different tone, a combination of amusement and surprise, said, 'I haven't been sightseeing for years.' Then in his more usual rather abrupt manner he went on, 'Where would you like to start?'

Happiness fizzed in Anya like champagne. 'You're the boss, on this occasion.' She grinned up at him. 'I leave it to you.'

His teeth flashed in the soft light. 'We'll have to discuss these feminist tendencies of yours,' he paused, 'some other time. Come on.'

They rode the Peak tram down to the central district then took a taxi out to West Point.

'This is one of the oldest parts of the colony.' Simon caught hold of her hand as the people crowding the narrow streets threatened to separate them, and Anya's pleasure was reinforced by the security of his warm grip. Tiny shops on the ground floors of tenement buildings three or four stories high spilled goods and customers out on to the road. Every building bristled with brightly painted signs in Chinese characters with translations in English and other languages from German to Arabic.

They looked into tailors' shops where a well-cut suit in English worsted or a cheongsam in silk-lined brocade with a beautiful beaded design could be made to measure in twenty-four hours at a ridiculously low price. There were shops selling curios and coffins; bamboo furniture; baskets; elaborate paper lanterns, hand painted and fringed with crimson tassels; carved candles of every size and colour.

Amid the crowds, manoeuvring their trays with great dexterity, the food vendors patrolled, selling peanuts, roasted chestnuts, hot soup, noodles and green tea. The appetising aromas mingled in the thick heat with the scents of burning joss sticks, rubber, dust, oil and sweating humanity.

'Where do all these people live?' Anya gasped, squeezing through the moving throng in Simon's wake, clinging tightly to his hand.

'Right here,' he indicated the tenements. 'One of

these buildings will house up to three hundred people.'

'But there can't possibly be that many rooms——'

'There aren't. Each room is divided into cubicles, *that's* what they rent. Then there could be another fifty people, plus chickens and ducks, living in huts on the roof as squatters.'

They moved along Hollywood Road. 'This is Man Mo Meal,' Simon said. 'It was built in 1848 and is the oldest Chinese Temple in the colony. Would you like to take a look? It's not a tourist temple, but visitors are allowed.'

Anya nodded and they went in. Sticks of incense burned in the perforated tops of polished brass urns on three-legged stands. There were crimson pillars and latticed screens. Wide stone steps led to a gold and crimson altar and above their heads hung large cones made from spirals of copper or bronze-coloured wire. The silence was broken only by the soft tinkle of wind-chimes.

Moved by an impulse Anya touched Simon's hand. 'May I light a joss stick?'

He raised one heavy brow. 'Why?' sounding more sceptical than surprised.

Anya wasn't sure herself. 'A token of respect.' She shrugged shyly.

'Go ahead.' He stood back watching without expression as she put some money into the black lacquered box and took one of the thin brown sticks. Holding it against one already burning she blew gently until the tip glowed red and fragrant smoke curled upward. Then she placed it alongside the others in the urn.

'Are you religious?' Simon was still sceptical.

'I don't go to church,' Anya replied, watching the wreathing smoke, 'but I believe there has to be something more than us. I think most people do, they just have different ways of expressing their beliefs and follow different routes in their search.'

She turned to face him, deeply shaken by the sudden realisation that despite her knowledge, her sophisticated training, she, brought up a Christian, was standing in a Chinese temple offering her small gift and her prayers to the ancient pagan gods, doing what countless women had done since time began. Sacrifices had been offered to the sun, laid at the feet of grotesque stone idols and serene golden Buddhas. Mystic symbols had been scratched in sun-baked earth, chants intoned over fires kindled from the twigs of special trees, and dances performed by moonlight at certain seasons. All with the same hope, the same yearning. Let him love me. Her need, her desire, was as ageless, as primitive as that of the ancient Egyptian princess, the Sioux maiden, or the Maori wahine.

'Shall we go?' she said brightly and without waiting walked out into the sunshine and noise.

He took her hand once more as they started down the worn stone steps of Ladder Street. The open-fronted shops had awnings to protect the displays from scorching sun or teeming rain which, in this season, occurred within minutes of each other. People surged around the displays of exotic fruits, vegetables, cheap jewellery, flowers, books and postcards; buying, haggling or just looking. Errand boys darted up and down on skinny legs with huge baskets, and an old street cleaner patiently brushed papers, plastic cups, bits of cardboard and rotten fruit towards his green and yellow cart.

'He'll have to do it all over again in five minutes,' Anya sympathised, watching people carelessly tossing empty sweet wrappers and cigarette packets where the sweeper had just cleaned.

Simon nodded. 'He's lucky. He fulfills a need. He had job security and no worry about where his next meal is coming from.' He leaned towards her, his eyes glinting. 'Be glad for him, not sorry.'

By the time they had battled their way into the Thieves Market, Anya was beginning to flag.

'Tired? Already?'

'I feel as though I've been through a siege.' Her smile was wry and self-mocking. 'I've never seen so many people. It is always like this?'

'Oh, no,' he said blandly, 'you wait till the tourist season, it gets quite crowded then. Come on, there's a really fascinating antique shop just along here. It's like looking at a slice of Chinese history, and you're here to learn.'

'Yes, sir,' Anya muttered rebelliously as he hustled her through the crush. The front was narrow but as they entered Anya could see the shop went back a long way. The walls were covered with carved and decorated spears. There was a set piece in one corner of the window, of cymbals with scarlet hand cords, black laquered drums, brass gongs and, supported from inside, a fiercely exotic Lion Dance costume.

In the opposite corner a mannequin was posed wearing a hip-length long-sleeved coat of black satin, richly embroidered with flowers and dragons in pink, cream and gold silk. Beneath it was an ankle-length skirt of scarlet brocade lavish with dragon motifs in gold thread. The headdress, sitting low on the forehead, was ornate, with scarlet ribbons, tassels, silk pom-poms and a curtain of tiny multi-coloured beads which covered the alabaster face with its finely drawn brows and tiny red mouth from forehead to throat.

'That looks a very splendid outfit,' Anya said admiringly. 'What's it for?'

'It's a traditional Chinese wedding dress,' Simon explained, waving the shop's proprietor away with a smile and a few words of Cantonese, the equivalent, Anya guessed, of 'we're just looking.' 'The Chinese adore colour, especially red, which signifies rejoicing. As in so many other countries, white is the colour of mourning, hardly suitable for a bride.'

They moved on. One glass cabinet contained a wood and metal opium pipe with its accoutrements of needle, resin cup and lamp. Another held some beautiful relief carvings in rich yellow metal. In a third lay an embroidered and tasselled hat of pink satin-brocade and matching miniature high-heeled boots for bound feet.

Anya's medical training made her all too aware of the agony high-born women must have suffered when as children their feet were tightly wrapped in wet bandages which restricted the blood supply and distorted the bones to produce the tiny arched foot traditionally prized as a mark of beauty and rank. She turned abruptly from the display to see Simon watching her.

'You must admit the workmanship is beautiful.'

'But the custom was barbaric,' she murmured angrily. 'Yet the Chinese had one of the earliest and richest civilisations. It doesn't make sense.'

'Is Western culture any less barbaric?' he countered. 'Victorian women did themselves appalling internal damage in their ridiculous desire for eighteen-inch waists. And today women get hepatitis from dirty tattoo needles, or disfiguring scars from lasers operated by incompetents in an effort to get rid of those same tattoos. Girls starve themselves into physical and mental illness in pursuit of an "ideal" shape which, in fact, flattens out all trace of femininity. Men have hair transplants and older women pay plastic surgeons to make their breasts larger, their buttocks smaller and to lift all signs of life and expression from their faces. Is it so different?'

Speechless, Anya stared at him. Then one corner of his mouth lifted and she couldn't help smiling. 'No, I suppose not,' she admitted. 'Funny how we rarely view our own behaviour with the same critical clarity we turn on everyone else's.'

'Let's have some lunch,' Simon suggested and they went out into the streets once more.

After their meal of crabmeat and sweet corn soup, sweet and sour pork with fried rice and two cups of green tea, Simon took Anya to the Tiger Balm Gardens, eight acres of grottoes and pavilions displaying effigies from Chinese mythology, with one particularly garish section depicting hell, He seemed to know all the legends and by the time they left Anya's head was reeling.

'What would you like to do now?' Simon asked.

Anya shook her head, laughing ruefully. 'I don't think I can absorb any more sights or culture. My brain feels like scrambled egg.'

'Come on. It's too early to go home yet. There must be something else you'd like to see.'

She looked sideways at him, diffidence replacing her smile. 'Well, not something exactly, someone.' Puzzlement drew Simon's brows together and Anya took a deep breath. 'Would you mind very much if we called at the hospital to see how Kam-Li is?' She rushed on, 'I know this is supposed to be a day off but I just . . .'

'Want to be sure the surgeon knows what he's doing,' Simon finished drily.

Anya blushed. 'I didn't mean it to sound like that.'

'Spare me your excuses, just tell me why.'

Anya struggled to find words to explain her confused feelings. She shrugged helplessly. 'I feel, sort of—involved, I suppose. Kam-Li was my first patient since starting this job. It's all so different from working in a big hospital. Besides, he's part of the crew and,' her cheeks were pink, 'we're much more dependent on one another out here, it's a bit like a family.' She lifted one shoulder, sure her explanation didn't make sense, yet not knowing how else to put it.

Simon eyed her thoughtfully. 'OK,' he said at last, 'the hospital it is.'

They followed the Chinese Staff Nurse down the long, crowded ward. Several beds were curtained off and it was in front of the second of these that she stopped. 'You may stay only a few minutes,' she warned. 'Mr Samanta operated this morning and the patient must rest.'

Anya masked a smile. The nurse's expression was severe and she obviously had the welfare of her patient at heart, yet the ward was a hive of activity, full of clatter and bustle with patients and staff chattering in loud voices. Quite how Kam-Li was supposed to rest in middle of it all was something of a mystery.

'Thank you, Staff. Is Mr Samanta still in the hospital?' Simon enquired.

'I imagine so.'

'Then would you be kind enough to ask him if he could spare me a moment?'

'Mr Samanta is an extremely busy man,' the nurse began, her expression lowering even further.

Simon cut in gently. 'I promise not to keep him long. Tell him it's Dr Simon Brody of the Floating Clinic Service. My colleague here is Dr Anya Lucas. The patient, Kam-Li, is employed on my boat.'

A variety of expressions chased across the nurse's

face. Then, swallowing, she murmured with a bright smile, 'Of course, Dr Brody,' and hurried away.

Anya parted the curtains and approached the bed. Kam-Li lay back on the pillows with both eyes heavily bandaged. She touched his hand. 'It's Dr Lucas, Kam-Li. Dr Brody's here too, he'll be along in a moment. How are you feeling?'

At the sound of her voice Kam-Li's lips parted in a smile. 'Dr Lucas? Is very kind you come. How long must I stay here?'

'Sim—Dr Brody is just checking on that. Is something wrong? Can't you sleep? It certainly is noisy in here.'

'The noise I don't mind. Is good to hear all the people and know what is happening even if I cannot see.'

Anya raised her eyebrows in silent question, as Simon entered the cubicle and after glancing quickly at Kam-Li's chart, went to the other side of the bed. He patted the young man's shoulder. 'Hello, Kam-Li. I've just spoken to Mr Samanta. He said the detachment was only partial and fortunately well away from the centre of your eye, so the operation has an excellent chance of complete success.'

The lower half of Kam-Li's face registered uncertainty. 'I will see again? As good as before?'

'Of course you will,' Simon reassured him.

'Didn't anyone explain about the operation? What it is and how it works?' Anya asked him. 'Don't shake your head,' she warned quickly.

'I intended to last night after I'd persuaded Samanta to put him on today's list,' Simon said quietly. 'But he'd been given analgesics and a sedative to help him sleep.'

'Everyone very busy,' Kam-Li said. 'No time to talk. Nurses say how many patients to look after.

Doctors come and go so fast, talk with each other.' He lifted one hand slightly and let it fall on to the bedcover again in resigned helplessness.

Anya felt a stab of anger. So the hospital was crowded and the staff overworked. But patients were expected to take far too much purely on trust. Kam-Li had a right to know what was happening to him. She looked across at Simon, her face mirroring her indignation.

One corner of his mouth tilted in a smile. 'Go ahead.'

Anya sat down on the side of the narrow bed. 'Kam-Li, do you remember on the boat I explained that the injury to your head had caused the inner lining of your eye to become separated from the underlying layer?'

'Yes.'

'Well, what Mr Samanta had to do was to anchor the inner layer, back on to its base.'

'But if he has done that why must I have these bandages on and lie so still?' Despite his efforts to hide it, frustration was evident in Kam-Li's tone.

'Because sudden movements or using the eye too soon can interfere with the healing process.'

'But,' Simon interjected, 'because your detachment was relatively small and at an easily reached site, you should have the bandages off your intact eye within a few days. Mr Samanta will examine your eye every day with a special instrument enabling him to see inside it and judge how quickly it is healing. You can ask him any questions and he will tell you whatever you want to know.' He motioned to Anya to stand up. 'We want you back on board one hundred per cent fit as soon as possible. So follow instructions and try to be patient. I know it won't be easy, but——' Simon broke off and pushed one curtain aside to peer down the ward. He raised a hand and beckoned to someone at the far end. 'You could be back on duty in less than a month. Dr Lucas and I have to go now, but you have another visitor.' He pulled the curtain aside and Susan Chang, blushing scarlet behind the huge bunch of flowers she held, edged into the cubicle.

Anya gave Susan a warm smile then turned back to Kam-Li and touched his shoulder. 'We'll see you soon.'

'Thank you, Dr Lucas, Dr Brody. Is very kind you come. I do what you say.' His voice trailed off and uncertainty turned down the corners of his mouth. 'Please, who is visitor?'

Anya glanced at Simon who put a finger to his lips and gave Susan a gentle push towards the bed. He slipped his other arm casually around Anya's shoulders and they watched as Susan murmured a greeting in Cantonese to Kam-Li. After a moment's silence, Kam-Li's mouth widened in a smile that stretched from ear to ear. His delight was undisguised as he held out a hand towards Susan, stumbling over his words, unexpectedly bashful. But as their fingers touched and entwined and she sat down timidly on the edge of the bed, his diffidence melted like snow in sunshine.

Simon let the curtain fall into place and with his arm still encircling her shoulders, guided Anya down the ward and out of the hospital.

'I didn't think you knew about them.' Anya was intensely aware of the warm weight of his arm, of his hip and thigh brushing hers as they walked. Her heart pounded unevenly.

He looked down, catching her eye. 'There isn't much I miss,' he said softly. Anya felt her throat and cheeks grow hot. Stepping in front of her so that she was forced to stop, he tilted her chin with his index finger, and there, in the middle of the hospital car park, Simon kissed her.

The gentle, demanding pressure of his lips made Anya's head swim. When at last he released her she stared at him, speechless, until she realised her heart was in her eyes. She looked down quickly.

'Let's go home,' he said.

It was almost six as they rode up the mountain in the tram. Heavy black clouds which had appeared out of nowhere burst open, the rain falling hard and fast, an opaque curtain blotting out the city below.

'What do you want to do?' Simon shouted above the hissing roar as they got off the tram. 'Wait it out or run for home?'

'How long is it likely to last?' Anya peered out. The deluge showed no sign of easing.

He shrugged. 'Anything from five minutes to an hour.'

Hang about there for an hour when they were only a few hundred yards from the house?

'Let's go,' she yelled and screwing up her eyes darted out of the terminal.

As they arrived at the gate breathless, and soaked to the skin, the clouds rolled away to reveal the sun, a huge orange ball low in the sky, its heat strong enough to start the road steaming at once.

Anya looked down at her saturated clothes then at Simon.

'Bloody typical,' he growled and they both burst out laughing. Simon shook his head sending a shower over Anya, who blinked. Droplets rolled down her face and she caught some on her tongue. Her hair was a mass of wet curls clinging to her scalp.

He closed the gate behind them. 'Ready?' He gestured for her to take his arm, then, with sandals squelching, to her utter amazement he began dancing her down the path as he belted out in a rich baritone, 'I'm sing-ing in the rain, just sing-ing in the rain . . .'

After a few speechless seconds Anya joined in improvising other steps as they cavorted up the path until, attempting an intricate double-shuffle, Simon tripped himself up and they arrived at the front doorstep in an undignified heap, both gasping with laughter.

Simon scrambled to his feet, his back to the door, holding out his hands to Anya. As she clasped them the door opened and she found herself looking at a pair of highly polished hand-made calf-skin shoes topped by fawn slacks with knife-edged creases. Her laughter faded as her glance took in the cream silk shirt and tie and the rich brown velvet jacket.

Seeing her expression change Simon looked over his shoulder.

'Charles!' Anya made no effort to hide her surprise. 'What are you doing here?'

'Anya, darling.' He leaned down and slid one hand under her arm, helping her to her feet and deftly drawing her away from Simon. Then he kissed her briefly on the mouth, an action which took her completely by surprise. 'I've come to take you out to dinner,' he announced smoothly.

'But how did you know? We didn't expect to be back today. If the vials hadn't been damaged . . . Oh, I'm sorry, have you two met?' She looked at Simon whose face had closed up and was now totally expressionless. Even worse, though he stood barely a foot away, he seemed to have withdrawn from her, from them, so completely she found it difficult to remember that only moments before this wary, watchful stranger had been dancing and singing, his laughter wrapping itself warmly round her heart.

'We've never been introduced,' Charles said, turning a supercilious smile on Simon who stared stonily back, 'though of course as Chief Medical

Officer and Administrator of the F.C.S., Dr Brody is frequently mentioned in the Medical Press,' he paused, 'and also in the society pages and gossip columns of our various newspapers.'

The antagonism between the two men was obvious and Anya began to feel uncomfortable. Why had Charles kissed her and called her 'darling'? He had never done so before. Theirs had never been that kind of relationship. And why was Simon suddenly so cold and aloof? She made the introduction. 'Simon, this is Charles Hagen, he's a plastic surgeon at the Private Hospital.'

'Hagen.' Simon nodded, shaking Charles's hand, the contact as brief as courtesy would permit. 'If you'll both excuse me, I'd like to change.' He eyed Charles. 'You must have been very persuasive to get past my housekeeper, Hagen.'

'No trouble at all, old boy,' he spread his hands. 'Not once she realised Anya and I were—good friends,' he smirked.

Anger flared in Anya. What was he doing? Obviously he had intimated they were far more than just friends, but why?

Simon's face was bleak and his eyes glittered like chips of topaz.

'I hope you haven't been exaggerating, Charles,' she said, keeping her voice cool, 'after all, we've hardly seen each other since Medical School.'

'Exactly.' He seized the initiative again. 'We've got such a lot to catch up on. You'd better get out of those wet clothes. Put on something pretty and I'll take you to the Hong Kong Hilton for the most delicious meal you have ever tasted.'

Anya glanced at Simon, doubt in her eyes, wishing he'd say something, anything.

Charles intercepted the look and went on, 'No need

to worry about the weather or that clanking tram, my Mercedes is parked just up the road. You'll travel in the style you deserve.' He smiled winningly. 'You have to come, Anya, with your erratic working hours, God knows when I'll catch you again.'

Still she hesitated, praying that Simon would say they had already made arrangements for the evening. But the truth was they hadn't. Then it occurred to her, maybe Simon had, but not with her. Perhaps that was the reason for his silence. But then he did speak, his voice cold and mocking.

'No, Anya, you can't turn an old friend down.'

He was telling her to go. He *wanted* her to go. She didn't understand. Pride came to her rescue. Chin high, her cheeks pink, she smiled at Charles. 'It sounds delightful. I'll be as quick as I can.' She turned to Simon, steeling herself against the sharp stab of pain. 'With your permission I'll ask Ah Mai to bring some tea.'

Simon raised a sardonic eyebrow. 'I'm sure Charles would prefer something a little stronger, wouldn't you, Charles?' His eyes never left Anya's and she hated him in that moment. They had been so close and now as if he had physically pushed her away, a great gap yawned between them. Why was he doing it? Surely he wasn't taking Charles's claims of close friendship seriously?

'Very civil of you, old boy,' Charles rubbed his hands together, 'a whisky wouldn't go amiss.'

'I'll see to it, Anya,' Simon drawled, motioning Charles to precede him into the drawing room. 'You'd better get ready.' His voice dropped so only she could hear it. 'Don't keep Prince Charming and his Mercedes waiting.'

Anya glared at him and biting back a furious retort, she whirled round and ran upstairs.

She didn't really want to go, couldn't he see that? She would much rather have spent the evening with him, talking over their day out, getting to know him better. Like her, he had begun to reveal more of his inner self, and like her, he was occasionally uncertain, tentative. Not that it ever showed in his voice or his manner, it was only a feeling she had. He always appeared commanding and in control. Except for the second night on the boat. His control had almost deserted him then. But that was different, any man would have reacted the way he did under the circumstances. It could be argued that what had happened was her own fault, that she was partially responsible.

But in her heart of hearts, she had known then and was even more certain now that what had drawn them together, had prompted him to kiss her, had fanned the flame of attraction into an inferno that had so nearly consumed them both, was not mere physical attraction and opportunity. It went much deeper than that. His physical strength and the unexpected force of her own feelings had frightened her and she had fought him. Yet voicing neither blame nor anger, he had held her hand, their fingers entwined, until she slept.

She loved him. He had an unusual way of looking at things. His views were often unexpected, jolting her out of a complacent rut of thinking she hadn't known she was in.

Why then? Why hadn't he stepped in and told Charles they were already doing something tonight? Why had he more or less pushed her into accepting Charles's invitation?

She paused in her drying, hugging the towel to her. Whatever he felt for her, and she had no way of knowing exactly what that was, there was already someone else in his life, Kerry.

Anya towelled her hair dry with unaccustomed vigour, resolving to put Simon out of her mind, at least for the evening. He did not want her company, Charles did, and they certainly had a lot to catch up on. If she could keep the conversation on their lives and work since leaving medical school, it should be quite a pleasant evening. The Hong Kong Hilton sounded both exotic and expensive, though money was the least of his worries if Charles's taste in clothes and cars was anything to go by.

Anya picked up the gold clutch bag that matched her sandals and studied her reflection in the long mirror. Her sleeveless dress of turquoise and pale green shot through with gold thread, a copy of a fabulously expensive Fortuny original, fell in hundreds of tiny pleats from a plain round neckline to just below her knees.

Her make-up was subtle, but the green and gold eyeshadow made her eyes look enormous, and the tawny-rose lipstick softened and warmed her mouth. Her hair had dried to a gleaming feathery cap curling softly across her forehead and round her ears. Gold stud earrings and an antique gold bracelet resembling a twisted rope were her only jewellery.

Her reflection stared back, objective, appraising, acknowledging her elegance with faint surprise. Oh Simon, she cried silently, why isn't this for you? She drew herself up, straightening her spine, squaring her shoulders. Because tonight, he didn't want her.

As she reached the bottom of the stairs Simon came out into the hall. They both froze as his gaze swept over her taking in her poise and the fine material of her dress clinging and fluid against her slender curves, shimmering in the soft light. For one breathless moment his eyes glittered fiercely and his features tightened with admiration and desire.

One word. That's all it would have taken. Just one word and she would have sent Charles on his way without shame or regret. She knew her eyes revealed what was in her heart but she did not care. Yet, still too unsure of herself, too afraid of rejection, of Simon's power over her, she could not speak.

The moment passed and Simon looked away, his face carefully blank. 'I'll tell him you're ready,' he said quietly.

Anya tilted her chin. Twin spots of colour high on her cheekbones were the only sign of the turmoil within her. 'Don't bother.' How did she manage to sound so cool, so casual? 'I'll tell him myself.' Head high she walked past Simon and into the drawing room.

It was the first time she had been in there. The colour scheme was the same as in the hall; jade, cream, ivory and gold. It suited the large room perfectly. The furniture, a mixture of styles, blended in gentle harmony, from the circular inlaid table, and the ivory chess set, each piece an intricately carved four-inch-high replica of ancient gods and goddesses, to the jade velvet chaise-longue.

Charles leapt to his feet, setting down his almost empty glass and pursing his lips in a low whistle of admiration. 'You look absolutely stunning.' His forehead creased as he eyed the dress. 'Say, that's not an original, is it?'

Charles certainly had an eye for quality and style. 'On my salary?' she smiled. 'Shall we go?'

Simon came out of his study as Anya re-entered the hall with Charles a few steps behind her. He had paused to finish the last of his whisky.

'You'll need this,' Simon held out a Yale key. 'That's for the front door. I'll leave the gate unlocked but remember to close the padlock when you come in.' There was no expression whatever in his voice.

Anya slipped the key into her purse. So many words trembled on the tip of her tongue and she dared not say any of them.

Charles put his arm round her shoulders in an overtly possessive manner. 'Don't wait up,' he grinned at Simon.

'I won't be late,' Anya said quickly.

'Hey, what is this?' Charles grimaced. 'Here I am with one of the most glamorous women in Hong Kong at my disposal and she's playing Cinderella. You're a big girl now, Anya, you don't need anyone's permission . . .'

He had gone far enough. Charles was deliberately trying to needle Simon whose rigid stance and poker face could not hide from Anya the fact that Charles was succeeding. 'I'm not asking permission,' she interrupted, 'we're leaving for the settlement again first thing in the morning and to do my job effectively, I need my sleep. Now, let's go.'

She wanted to get away. Away from the house where, despite his obvious wealth and style, Charles did not fit, grating on the tranquil atmosphere like a rusty nail on glass. Away from the man she loved, who did not love her and who had more or less forced her into this evening out with someone she had not seen for years and who, for reasons of his own, was behaving with unexpected and discomfiting familiarity.

Once in the sleek silver-grey car, Charles seemed to relax. He was a good driver, if a little flashy, and obviously knew the island well, pointing out the homes of people important in the colony as they followed the winding road down into the city.

Once they were seated in the air-conditioned opulence of the Jade Lotus, the Hong Kong Hilton's speciality Chinese Restaurant, Anya tried to steer

Charles away from tit-bits of gossip concerning the various prominent people. She sensed he was leading up to telling her things about Simon and from the way the two men had reacted in each other's company, they would not be pleasant or complimentary, and she did not want to hear. She was learning about Simon in her own time and her own way. Anything Charles told her would be irrelevant.

'Do you go sailing much, Charles? I remember you used to be very keen at university.'

'I belong to the Yacht Club, of course, but I don't get out on the water very often. Actually, I'm a member of the Jockey Club as well.' He paused after this announcement, obviously waiting for her reaction.

'Oh? How interesting.' Anya smiled. 'Do you ride instead then?'

Charles shook his head with condescending patience. 'You haven't a clue, have you? Haven't your horizons widened at all? There is more to life than just work, you know.'

'Yes, I do know,' Anya said quietly, remembering the talks she'd had with Simon, and their day of sight-seeing. She wrenched her attention back to Charles. 'So, what is special about belonging to the Jockey Club if you don't ride?'

His smile radiated self-satisfaction. 'Prestige. For a start, one has to have a certain social and financial standing before one's name can even be put forward for election and even then the selection procedure can be pretty damn tricky. But once you are a member it opens a lot of very useful doors. The Jockey Club controls the Hong Kong Racecourse. I don't suppose you've seen it yet?' Anya shook her head. 'It's up in Happy Valley. Of course racing takes place in the winter when it's dry. The season starts in early October. You must come to the opening meeting as my guest. I'll introduce you to some useful people. We have three sweepstakes each season and the first prize is worth well over a million Hong Kong dollars.' He examined his fingernails. 'Brody isn't a member, of course.' He glanced up from under sandy brows, watching her closely.

'Really.' Anya wondered what Charles was hinting at, then decided she didn't want to know. Simon probably didn't have either the time or the inclination to join clubs. He'd even turned down an invitation to a Reception at Government House, and from the way he'd done it it was not the first time. For an instant Anya was tempted to ask Charles if he'd been invited, but she resisted. It would serve no purpose.

'You know that we in the Jockey Club help fund Brody's outfit, the Floating Clinic Service?' Charles said.

Anya nodded. 'An infinitely worthwhile cause.' She grinned impishly, 'Though as I now work for Si—for the F.C.S. you could say I'm biased.'

The waiter cleared away their soup bowls and brought in the next course of lightly steamed fish with a dressing of garlic, green onions, chives, ginger, sugar and soy sauce.

How Charles had changed. Money seemed to rule his life. Its acquisition, what it would buy, its influence in helping him climb the social ladder. 'Useful' was the measure by which he appeared to judge everything, from people to social activities. Why? His family were quite well-off, so it wasn't as if he'd ever been denied anything and was now determined to make up for it.

Anya sipped her white wine and couldn't help wondering why he had insisted on bringing her out to dinner. She was a newcomer to Hong Kong. Of what possible 'use' could she be? Then she felt ashamed.

She was being rude and unkind. 'Tell me about your work, Charles. I've read of some amazing developments in microsurgery techniques for correcting birth defects in children.'

He nodded, waving the waiter away, and serving himself, 'Yes, I've read some of the articles.'

Anya was puzzled. 'You don't sound very interested.'

'Why should I be?' He shrugged. 'There's not much call for that sort of work out here. Besides, you have to be realistic. Medicine is a business, and to be successful in any business you have to make money.' He swallowed a mouthful of food and offered Anya more wine. She shook her head and he filled his own glass. 'That's how you're judged, you know. That's how society labels the successes and the failures, it's all in the bank balance.' He leaned back and raised his glass. 'Well, yours truly is doing very nicely, thank you. There are a lot of wealthy people in Hong Kong whose appearance is extremely important to them. For example, a man works for twenty years to build up a business, the profits are rising, everything looks good, except him. He's got experience, talent and years of active life ahead of him, but the years of effort have left their mark—pouches under the eyes, frown lines and a chin that hangs in folds. Some discreet surgery and that same man looks twenty years younger, and because he's happier with himself he radiates confidence and as a result his business flourishes.'

Anya toyed with her glass. 'Yes, but——'

Charles continued as though she hadn't spoken. 'What's so great about looking old? Age is disfiguring. I tell you, Anya, I've had women in their forties come into my office depressed to the point of suicide because of the lined face and sagging body they see in the mirror each morning. But six weeks after surgery there's a new spring in their step. They walk taller, wear their clothes with more pride, make a positive statement about their existence. Their husbands suddenly wake up to the fact that the wife they've either ignored for years or taken for granted, is a damned attractive woman. Yes,' he leaned back in his chair and swirled the wine round in his glass, 'I'd say, in all modesty, I'm one of the most sought-after surgeons in Hong Kong.'

Anya recalled Simon's description of the work done in the rehabilitation hospital for lepers. The surgeons working round the clock to repair the ravages of the disease and restore useful function to deformed limbs.

'In fact,' Charles was saying, 'surgery is only one aspect of my job, I'm psychologist, counsellor and confidante as well, and it's damned exhausting sometimes, I can tell you.'

Anya put her fork down carefully and dabbed her mouth with her napkin. 'Charles, don't you feel sometimes that . . .' she hesitated, 'well, that perhaps your talents as a surgeon could be put to better use?'

He stared at her for a moment then began to laugh. '*Better* use? Anya, I'm one of the best there is, and because I'm good I can charge whatever I want and still have a waiting list four months long.'

'That wasn't exactly what I meant——' she began.

'I know it wasn't.' His smile faded and a frown took its place. 'I've worked damned hard for what I've got, Anya.' He tossed back the last of his wine and poured himself another glassful.

'I don't doubt that, Charles, but——' Anya stopped, looking down at her plate. She wasn't sure she had the right to ask, yet something was wrong.

'But what?'

'Why aren't you happy, Charles?' She put the question softly.

His eyebrows lifted in atonishment. 'Not happy? Who's not happy?' Then he looked away, studying the wine as he turned his glass round and round. 'You know those parties so beloved by the gossip columnists, an "intimate bash for five hundred friends"? I get invited to all those. I have a penthouse flat and a brand new Mercedes and I'm totally free of all commitments and responsibilities. No parents, brothers or sisters living down the road and bothering me with their problems. No wife waiting at home to hear about my day. There are plenty who'd like to be in my shoes.' He raised the glass to his lips and took a long swallow.

'So maybe the work isn't as challenging as it once was,' he seemed almost to be talking to himself, 'and maybe I do sometimes wonder if what I'm doing is really worthwhile.' He drained his glass and looked directly at her, his mouth widening in a smile that never reached his eyes. 'But we're all in cages of one kind or another, aren't we?' He leaned back in his chair and with a visible effort, banished the doubts. 'Hey, what am I saying? I make a very comfortable living, doing a job I'm good at, for which there is a demand. What more could a man want?'

'What indeed?' Anya smiled, feeling unaccountably sorry for him.

'Now,' he said briskly, 'I want to hear about you. What brought you to these shores? I thought you had your feet firmly on the career ladder at Heathfield?'

'So did I,' she agreed and as the waiter brought an exotic fruit salad she began to tell Charles about the circumstances that had decided her to reorganise her life. But while she talked part of her mind detached itself from the conversation and observed. How different he was from Simon. It wasn't just the money. To live where he did Simon had to be reasonably well off, not that you'd guess it from his clothes, and if he had a car he certainly didn't use it much. No, it was their approach to life that divided them, set them poles apart. Charles gave the *impression* of being interested in his clients—you couldn't call them patients for they weren't ill. He claimed to enjoy his life but the tension that showed itself in nervous mannerisms and in the amount he was drinking, denied his words.

Simon, doing the jobs of two men, was plainly overworked, yet not the smallest detail regarding his patients was overlooked. Last night he had made a point of going to see Kam-Li in the hospital, though as a patient Kam-Li was no longer under their care. Anya recalled the glow on Madam Sen's lined face when she spoke of the help Simon had given her. In Charles' view wrinkles and lines were disfiguring, but to Anya they were a mark of one woman's extraordinary courage under appalling suffering; revealing pride, humility and above all, character. To erase them would be to deny her life and all she had experienced. Then there was Pixie. Anya had dealt with enough children to realise their instincts were seldom wrong. They could see beyond smiles. Being a woman had supposedly given her a link with the little Chinese girl, yet she had to admit that though Pixie had accepted her, she had responded much more freely and happily to Simon. Despite being a very private man he had an empathy with people of all ages that Anya could only envy.

'. . . you really ought to see it,' Charles was saying. Anya couldn't remember drinking her coffee, yet the empty cups were there in front of them and Charles had summoned the waiter and was paying the bill.

'I'm sorry,' she blinked, 'I didn't catch what you said.'

'I was inviting you back to my place for a nightcap.'

Charles smiled winningly. 'The penthouse has one of the best views on the Island, far better in my opinion than the Peak. Of course, I had to pay way over the market price to get it, but it was worth every penny. I think you'll be impressed.' He leaned towards her. 'And to celebrate our reunion, I've got a bottle of Dom Perignon on ice.'

Anya glanced at the clock on the far wall. Ten o'clock. Thank goodness. 'Charles, I'd have liked nothing better, but it's late and I really must get back.'

Frown lines formed and deepened between his brows. 'Late? What are you talking about? The evening's barely started.'

'For you, maybe,' Anya smiled to soften the rejection, 'but my week has been really hectic and we're off again early tomorrow morning.'

She could see he wanted to argue, to persuade her to change her mind. 'I'm sorry, Charles,' she picked up her bag and pushed back her chair, 'but I really do have to go. I need all the sleep I can get.'

He held her chair, then took her arm to escort her out. 'Perhaps next time.' He squeezed her arm. The *maitre d'* inclined his head, wished them both a good evening and hoped everything had been to their satisfaction. Charles assured him it had, and they went out into the foyer. The car was brought round. Charles tipped the boy and helped Anya in. Next time. He went round to the driver's seat and the powerful car purred away from the hotel. Did she want a next time?

'When will you be free again?' Charles asked, swinging into the traffic. 'How long are you likely to be away at this settlement?'

'I don't know.' At least she could answer that with total honesty. 'It seems the usual rotas and timetables have been abandoned while these vaccine tests are going on.'

'Then you should have quite a bit of free time due when the tests are over.' Charles had his foot down hard on the accelerator, weaving between lanes, driving fast.

Anya felt all her muscles tighten up. She didn't want to hurt his feelings, but neither did she wish to give him any encouragement. 'We're understaffed for the amount of work involved, so it's possible we'll just press on. Charles, would you mind slowing down a little.'

He glanced across at her. 'But I thought you were anxious to get back.' There was an edge to his voice.

'I'd rather be a little late and all in one piece,' she smiled.

Charles glowered out of the windscreen. 'Brody has no right to push you like that. You're entitled to proper time off.'

'He's not pushing me, Charles. I knew what I was getting into when I took the job.' She mentally crossed her fingers to cancel the lie. 'Besides I've never been a nine-to-five person, and I'm enjoying the challenge.'

He braked and the car squealed to a stop outside the wrought iron gate.

Anya breathed a quiet sigh of relief and unclenched her hands. 'Thank you for a lovely evening, Charles.' She rested her fingers on the door handle. 'The meal was delicious and I've enjoyed catching up.'

'You know what, Anya?' There was bitterness in his laugh as he turned towards her, sliding his arm along the back of her seat, 'That sounds suspiciously like a brush-off.'

'No,' she said quickly, taken by surprise, then wished she hadn't denied it, for if she were honest, it was. Charles had changed. She barely recognised her friend from Medical School. She had changed as well, probably more than she realised, and especially since coming to Hong Kong, since meeting Simon. Whatever she and Charles had once had in common, it had long since evaporated, burned away by his ambition to make money, and her search for fulfilment. There was really no point in meeting again.

'Don't fake it, Anya,' he said softly. 'I don't need charity, yours or anyone else's.'

'Charles . . .' She turned towards him, aware of how much she loved Simon and how, despite all he had, Charles seemed suddenly so lonely.

He looked up, a half-smile curving his mouth. 'A goodbye kiss? For old times' sake?'

Before Anya could move, his arm slid from the back of the seat and clamped around her shoulders, pressing her against him and his lips, hot and moist and tasting of brandy, fastened on hers.

For an instant Anya was shocked into immobility as she realised his wry acceptance had been merely a pose. The pressure of his lips forced hers apart and his tongue lancing into the softness of her mouth galvanised her into action. She began to struggle, but that inflamed him further. He held her so tightly she could hardly breathe and ran his free hand down her throat, her shoulder, her bare arm and across the swell of her breast. His breathing was fast and loud.

Anya fought furiously, pushing his probing fingers away, then before he could grab her flailing arm, she slapped his face with all the force she could muster. The sound echoed through the car like a pistol shot. Charles released her at once, clapping his hand to his cheek as he sat back. They were both panting.

'You bitch,' he gasped.

Anya was trembling violently, as much from a sense of having been betrayed as from anger. 'And you, Charles?' She reached for the door handle, hurling the words at him with icy contempt, 'How would you describe your behaviour?' She climbed out of the car and slammed the door, clutching at the roof as she willed her legs to stop shaking and support her. The electric window hummed down.

'Guess I arrived too late.' Charles had recovered quickly, and his face at the open window was distorted by a sneer. 'I should have known you were playing for higher stakes when you told me you were staying with Brody instead of at an hotel.'

'What are you talking about? I explained the reasons for that.'

'Don't play innocent with me, Anya. You're only turning me down because you think you're on to something better.'

The colour drained from Anya's face then flooded back in a tide. She felt dizzy with the force of her anger. 'Why, you conceited——'

He didn't let her finish. 'You're not the first to make that mistake, but none of the others got him to the altar either. Just remember that, doll-face. And another thing, my money is clean, every last cent of it earned by my own talents as a surgeon. There are no skeletons in my closet, no dark shadows in my past.' He withdrew his head and started the engine.

Anya bent down, holding the door with both hands. 'What do you mean? What are you saying?'

'I guess you haven't been here long enough to find out, so I'm doing you a favour.' He gesticulated wildly at the house and garden behind the wrought iron gate. 'Do you have any idea how much a place like this costs? Haven't you ever wondered where his money comes from? Simon Brody, saviour of sick peasants, a shining example to us all.' Charles's eyes glittered feverishly and Anya flinched at his bitter sarcasm.

'All right,' her voice was barely audible, 'whatever it

is that's poisoning you, Charles, say it and go. Where does Simon's money come from?'

'Drug running.' Charles watched her avidly, his satisfaction blatant as she gasped. 'Sleep well, sweetheart.' The sleek car roared up the road leaving Anya staring after it in frozen disbelief.

Somehow she reached the front door and was fumbling for the key Simon had given her when it swung open and he stood silhouetted in the light from the hall.

She stared up at him. It couldn't be true. Not drug running. Not *Simon*. Something of her horror and confusion must have shown on her face for he took a step towards her, concern drawing his black brows together. 'Anya? What's the matter?' His face hardened. 'Hagen, didn't—give you any trouble, did he?'

She forced a smile, but the muscles in her cheeks were so stiff and her mouth so numb, she knew it must look ghastly. 'Of course not, I'm just tired. It's all caught up on me at once. We've been so busy and what with the heat . . .' She was babbling and her voice was that of a stranger, bright and brittle. She went to pass him but he caught her shoulders and pulled her round, his face dark with anxiety. 'What is it, Anya? What's happened? My God, if Hagen's tried anything . . .'

'Stop it,' she cried, wrenching herself free, turning on him like a wounded animal. 'I don't know what caused the war between you two, I don't want to know, but I'm not part of it and I won't be used to settle old scores.' She ran up the stairs.

'Anya, wait!' Simon started after her, but she flung her arm back, waving him away. Reaching her room she slammed the door and locked it, leaning against the cool wood, clasping her arms across her breasts as tremors shook her from head to foot.

## CHAPTER SEVEN

SHE must have slept, Anya supposed, but there was no respite from her tortured thoughts. They had pursued her, closing in from all sides until trapped, beaten, she had started running, faster and faster. She tripped and began to fall, down and down into blackness. The echoes of her own scream woke her.

She sat up in bed, her thin cotton nightie sticking clammily to her, her heart thudding against her ribs. At once the doubts and denials began raging once more. She clasped her head in her hands, resting her elbows on her knees. How could she believe it? Yet Charles would not have invented such a story, no matter how much he disliked Simon. Why *did* he hate Simon so much? If it was true, was it in the past or was Simon still involved?

Images of Madam Sen and Pixie flashed before her eyes. Simon caring, Simon a drug runner. How could she ever reconcile the two? And where did *she* stand? Could she go on loving a man who healed on one hand and traded death with the other? Could she stop loving him? The night seemed endless.

When the first pale rays of dawn lightened the eastern sky, Anya got up and crept into the shower. The warm, needle-sharp spray refreshed her body and calmed her mind. They were going back to the settlement. She had a job to do. She had to concentrate all her energy on the people who needed her professional help and put her personal problems aside. She could not allow them to overwhelm her, no matter how they threatened.

She was first and foremost a doctor. That had been her rule since qualifying. Only since coming to Hong Kong had she allowed the fact of being a woman to equal her commitment to medicine, only since meeting Simon Brody. And the result? Devastation. Somehow she would have to face Simon with what Charles had told her. She would be risking not only her job but her whole happiness, yet the questions had to be asked. But when, and how?

Back in her room she tried to disguise the ravages of the night with make-up, but nothing could hide the dark smudges beneath her eyes or the way her skin stretched tautly over her high cheekbones. She packed spare trousers and T-shirts, all freshly washed and ironed by Ah Mai, then added underwear and some books. Then, all too soon, it was time to go down for breakfast. The thought of food revolted Anya, yet she knew her nerves desperately needed nourishment if she was to cope with the emotional ordeal of living and working with Simon while coming to terms with her new knowledge and deciding how best to deal with it.

He was sitting on one of the chrome and leather stools at the breakfast bar, his sandalled feet hooked over the lower rung. The pale blue T-shirt, stretching like a second skin across his broad shoulders, had come loose from the belt of his faded jeans. Both elbows rested on the bar as he supported his forehead with one hand, engrossed in a report.

Though she was prepared and had steeled herself against it, at the sight of him her heart swelled as though it would burst. Oh God, I love him so much, she cried silently, what am I going to do?

The sound of her entrance brought his head round but his smile of greeting faded and his eyes narrowed. Quickly she looked away, crossing to the fridge to pour herself some chilled fruit juice. 'Good morning,' she said brightly, her back to him. 'Isn't it a lovely day? A bit hazy perhaps but maybe that will clear. What's the forecast? Any more typhoons floating around?' Shut up, *shut up*, she berated herself savagely, you sound totally artificial. Try and act normally. But what is more normal than for English people to talk about the weather? Anya swallowed the lump in her throat. What was normal about this whole situation?

From the corner of her eye she saw him swivel round to face her. 'As a matter of fact there was a warning issued at six a.m. this morning, but I think we'll reach the settlement in plenty of time.' His tone did not alter. 'What's wrong, Anya, and don't tell me "nothing". I'm neither blind nor stupid.'

She drank the last of her juice and replaced the glass on the work-top, gripping it tightly to stop her hand shaking. 'I didn't sleep too well,' she tried to sound off-hand, 'I guess I was a bit over-tired, nothing to make a fuss about.'

'You're lying to me,' he said quietly and there was a sadness in his voice that tore at her. 'Why, Anya?'

She couldn't bear it. She'd tell him now, get it all into the open, hurl Charles's accusations at him and watch his reaction. Then she knew she couldn't. This wasn't the time or the place. They'd have to leave for the dock in a few minutes. She swung round on him. 'What do you want me to say?' she demanded, her hands clenched, white-knuckled at her sides. 'I had a restless night, bad dreams, I'm tired, I——' She bit her lip and took a deep, shuddering breath. 'I'm sorry, I . . .'

The 'phone rang and Simon got up to answer it. As he took the receiver off the wall he pointed to the cereal packet and the toast, 'Eat,' he commanded.

Anya crossed the kitchen and was about to sit down

when Simon took the receiver from his ear and held it out. 'For you,' he said briefly, a tiny muscle jumping at the point of his jaw.

Too preoccupied to wonder or even care who it might be, Anya took the receiver, watching Simon's back as he returned to his seat. 'Hello? Dr Lucas here.'

'Anya, what can I say?'

At the sound of Charles's voice Anya stiffened. Automatically she glanced at Simon but he appeared to be totally immersed in the report, making notes in one of the margins. She could not see his expression, a mask of bleak anguish as he stared sightlessly at the nonsensical marks made by a pen gripped between nerveless fingers.

'I think you said it all,' she replied quietly and started to replace the receiver.

Charles must have sensed her intention. 'Wait. For God's sake, don't hang up,' he shouted, 'there's something I have to tell you.'

Anya put the 'phone to her ear once more, her heart pounding so hard she could barely hear him. Had it been a lie? A silly, vicious lie? Please, oh please let him say he'd lied. She struggled to keep her voice cool and even. 'What is it, Charles?'

'Look—last night—I was canned. I've had a few problems this week, nothing desperate, but time-consuming and time is money, you know how it is. So I was tired and a bit down and I drank too much. The thing is—I guess I read more into our getting together again than was actually there and, seeing you with Brody, dancing up the path—God-dammit, you both looked so happy. It hit me hard. You see he was the cause of a break-up between me and someone I was very fond of. Kerry was quite a bit younger than me, but——'

The name hit Anya like a slap in the face. Kerry. It

wasn't that common and given that Simon had broken up Charles's romance, the Kerry in question could only be the girl who though now in Switzerland, had a room of her own in Simon's house.

'Anya? Are you still there?' Charles's voice came down the wire, anxious, apologetic.

'Yes,' she whispered, then clearing her throat repeated it more loudly.

'So will you forgive me? It was inexcusable I know but I swear to God, I don't usually go on like that. Anya, please?'

'All right, Charles,' she said softly, then gripping the receiver in both hands, she swallowed the dryness in her throat. 'Charles,' her gaze flickered towards Simon. He still had his back to her but there was an unnatural rigidity about him. She sensed from his very stillness that he was listening. How could she phrase the question she desperately needed to ask so that Simon would not know, could not guess, what she was talking about.

'Charles,' she began again, 'you gave me some information last night. You are certain it's accurate?'

'You mean about Brody?'

'Yes.'

Charles's voice came back flat and metallic through the ear-piece. 'You don't think I'd lie about a thing like that, do you? Look, it must be hard to stomach, but at least you've found out in time. I mean you haven't been here long enough to get involved or anything . . .'

'Thank you, Charles,' she cut him off, hope draining away leaving behind only cold emptiness.

'Look,' Charles hurried on, 'I'll ring you when you get back. I want to make amends. We'll go to a show, one of the new nightclubs, something special.'

'I have to go,' Anya said tonelessly, 'goodbye,

Charles.' He was still talking when she replaced the receiver. Mechanically she buttered a slice of toast, spread lime marmalade on it and ate it, but it might just as well have been cardboard for all she could taste. The coffee, hot and strong, warmed her and she felt a little better. Life had to go on and now she knew the worst.

The 'phone rang again. Simon looked up from his report. 'Are you expecting another call?' His voice was carefully neutral. 'Do you want to take it?'

She shook her head. 'No,' she said firmly.

Simon gave a brief nod then picked up the 'phone. Anya finished her coffee as Simon's voice changed from an abrupt 'Hello,' to a delighted 'What? When? That's marvellous news. You are sure about the date? In two weeks? Make it the Saturday and I'll try and arrange to be free. Yes, I'll tell them. Now get off the 'phone, I have to go to work.' There was a pause and glancing sideways as she took her dishes to the sink, Anya saw Simon smiling broadly, his lips parted to reveal strong white teeth, laughter lines creasing the tanned skin at the corner of his eyes as he listened.

In that instant she knew who was calling and leaned against the work-top, her back to him, crushed by this second blow.

'All right, no, I won't forget,' she heard him say, his tone one of fond exasperation. 'It's just the way you left it—well, almost. No, I don't have time to explain now.'

Her eyes scalding with unshed tears, Anya turned to leave the kitchen. She kept her head down and pushed past Simon who put out an arm to stop her.

'See you in a fortnight,' she heard him say as she went out into the hall. 'Take care and don't overdo the farewell party. Bye.' The 'phone crashed back on to its rest and the kitchen door was wrenched open. 'Anya?'

But she fled upstairs. Blinking away the tears and fastening her lower lip between her teeth to stop it trembling, she made space among her clothes for her toilet bag, then zipped the holdall shut. She drew a deep breath and took a quick, critical look in the mirror. She had spent most of her adult life hiding her feelings. Never had it been more vital or more difficult than now.

'Anya?' Simon tapped on her door. She opened it, slinging the strap of her bag over one shoulder as she hefted the holdall in her other hand.

'I'm ready.' She didn't look at him. 'Are we going straight to the dock by taxi, or on the Peak tram to the centre?'

He seemed momentarily perplexed, as if his thoughts were elsewhere 'Oh, by tram. Sure you've got everything? Here, let me.' He took the holdall and picked up his own which he'd dropped by the stairhead, then followed her down.

Anya heard the sound of a key in the back door and Ah Mai trotted out of the kitchen. She bowed a greeting, her wrinkled walnut face beaming. Anya attempted a smile and a few words in Cantonese while Simon dropped both holdalls and strode into his study, returning a moment later with his briefcase.

'Kerry is coming home in two weeks,' he told the tiny Chinese woman who squeaked with pleasure, clapping her hands against her cheeks.

'I'll move out as soon as we return from this trip.' Anya directed the words at the housekeeper who looked startled.

'*Doh um geeh*? Solly, pardon?' She repeated.

'What are you talking about?' Simon cut in, frowning.

Anya took refuge in formality. 'I'm most grateful for your kindness.' Her heartache was a physical pain.

'But I really do think it's time I found somewhere of my own.'

Ah Mai babbled in quick-fire Cantonese, her small face puckered in bewildered astonishment.

Simon made a brief reply but her eyes never left Anya. 'Why do you talk of leaving?' he demanded. 'We've been through all this once.'

'Yes, but it's different now.' Surely he must understand she could not stay?

'Don't you like being here?' His voice was very low.

She was agonised. 'That has nothing to do with it. Kerry's coming home.'

'Yes, but what has *that* to do with anything?' Simon looked puzzled.

Anya felt a pang of anger. She was trying to do the right thing, discreetly and with the minimum of fuss, and he was not helping at all, in fact he was being positively obstructive. 'For a start I'm in her room.'

Simon looked relieved and began to laugh. 'Oh, is that what's bothering you. You're probably right, Kerry is rather possessive about that room. Ah Mai will move your things into one of the guest rooms. There are two, one looking out over the front garden and the other with windows on to the side and back. Which would you prefer?'

Anya stared at him. How could he? She had thought him intuitive, perceptive, but right now he seemed totally oblivious to her embarrassment and misery. Her frustration spilled over and without thinking she blurted, 'Don't be ridiculous.'

His face hardened. 'I beg your pardon?'

'It should be perfectly obvious why I can't stay.'

He took a step towards her. Ah Mai watched them both, her boot-button eyes bright with curiosity. 'It isn't obvious to me,' he said quietly. 'Unless Hagen has offered an alternative you prefer?'

'No.' Anya's denial was immediate and emphatic.

'Then as far as I'm concerned the reasons for your coming here in the first place are still valid, though you didn't answer my question.'

'What question?'

'Don't you like it here?'

'You know I do, but——'

'Then nothing has changed. Now let's get going. We have to stop off at the Pharmacy to pick up the new batch of vaccine. While I'm seeing to that, I want you to call in at the office and collect copies of the schedules for the next three weeks. I'll have to meet Kerry at the airport and I guess I ought to take a couple of days off to help her get settled again. Thank God you're here to take some of the load.'

Riding down in the tram they were both preoccupied with their own thoughts. In her mind Anya went over the things he had said. Nothing had changed. Couldn't he see that for her *everything* had changed? No, of course he couldn't, she had hidden it too well. Thank goodness she had. If she had let slip that she loved him, the situation would be unbearable. For much of the time she had managed to put Kerry out of her mind. Of course she had known the girl would come home sometime, but Anya had not imagined it would be quite so soon. Yet Simon's attitude was quite odd. He had been plainly delighted with the news but less than ecstatic at the prospect of taking two days off to welcome Kerry back.

And what about *her* position? What was she to do? He was quite adamant about her staying, but was that simply because he knew she had nowhere else to go and felt responsible for her?

She loved the house and Ah Mai seemed to have accepted her, even welcomed her. But how could she stay and watch Simon talking, sharing meals and private jokes with another woman—his mistress. Maybe for him the issue was simple, clear-cut. Kerry was part of his personal life, while she, Anya, belonged to his professional world. Sharing the cabin had clouded the issue a little and the demarcation lines had become blurred. But they were both free adults and Kerry was away, so where was the harm? Was that how he saw it? And hovering in the background, casting an oppressive shadow, was the dark spectre of Charles's revelation that Simon's money came from drug running.

Was love really blind? Was that why she found it so hard to accept? She could not bear to think of giving up her job, but she would have to leave the house. She needed space between them and time to think, to sort out the terrible confusion in her mind and her tangled feelings. On their return from this trip he was certain to call at the hospital to check on Kam-Li's progress. She would go on back to the house, pack the remainder of her things and slip away to an hotel before he returned. She'd have to leave a note, she owed him that. But what to say? And as she wrestled with that problem another one intruded, even more urgent. Tonight they would be sharing the cabin again.

The boat was under way. Simon was in theatre working on the operating light which needed adjustment. Susan was loading the steriliser with instruments and fresh dressing packs. She was still obviously concerned about Kam-Li.

Carol looked pale and drawn. When Anya had entered the consulting room ahead of Simon who had gone to see the Captain, Carol had been coming out of the dispensary and had jumped like a scalded cat.

'Oh, Dr Lucas, I wasn't—I mean, I didn't hear you

come in, you made me jump,' she added unnecessarily, her mouth stretched in a travesty of a smile.

'Are you all right?' Anya frowned in concern. 'You look a bit under the weather.'

'Me? No, I'm fine,' Carol assured her, then seeing Anya's obvious doubt she amended, 'I—er—had a slight stomach upset, but I'm quite all right now.' She added hastily, 'It won't affect my work, I promise.'

Anya decided to let the matter rest, but to keep an eye on the young nurse. She felt there was more behind the girl's stretched nerves and sick pallor than a simple digestive upset. But as long as she worked efficiently it might be more tactful to wait until they returned to Victoria before pressing for explanations.

With no particular duties until they arrived at the settlement, Anya went to the cabin and unpacked her few things, more aware than ever of how small it was, and how close the bunks were. She snatched up the book on traditional Chinese remedies Simon had loaned her and returned to the dispensary. Opening the tall cupboard at the end she began taking down the jars and bottles one at a time, looking for their contents in the book and started to memorise the ailments for which they were used, the method of making them up and the frequency of dosage or application. As always, immersing herself in work enabled her to step aside from the fears and worries that plagued her. She had been busy for an hour when Simon walked in. 'What are you doing?'

She lifted the book. 'Expanding my knowledge. I had no idea that the wind anemone had so many applications; earache, joint pains, not to mention——'

'I have read the book,' he interrupted drily. 'If you can spare half an hour I'd like you to check the date codes on the controlled drugs.' He tossed her his key which she caught deftly. 'When I was at the Pharmacy, Robert reminded me we haven't done our six-monthly check. Susan or Carol can do the other stuff later.'

Anya returned the tall jar to the shelf and closed the book. 'I'll start right away.'

Simon nodded and made for the door. On the threshold he turned. 'You and I have some talking to do,' he said quietly, 'but it can wait till tonight. Once we turn in and that cabin door is shut there'll be nowhere for you to run to.' He went out leaving Anya staring at the doorway, her heart hammering and her knees weak.

Moving like a sleepwalker she unlocked the C.D. cupboard. As the doors swung open she wrenched her attention back to the job in hand.

Starting on the left side of the top shelf she began checking the Class A drugs, highly addictive and dangerous narcotic analgesics. The ampoules and strip-packed tablets were contained in white boxes marked with broad bands or squares of colour for easy identification. After examining the seal and date stamp on each box, she returned it to its place on the shelf, straightening the rows as she moved along.

Phenazocine, morphine and pethidine were all within the coded date. Then she came to the heroin. The five boxes were there, just as Simon had said. Anya lifted them down and examined the first one. As was customary, the new boxes had been placed at the back and the older ones moved forward to be used first. The seal on the first box was broken and opening it Anya saw that two ampoules had been taken out. She checked the register: the two ampoules had been signed out by Simon the previous week for a patient named Wang Cheung. Anya replaced the lid on the box and put it to one side. She hesitated for a moment then walked swiftly out into the consulting room and pulled open the drawer in the filing cabinet which held the treatment sheets.

She hated having to do it, but knew there was no way she could justify *not* checking. The sheets were filed in alphabetical order, but none carried the name she sought.

A memory sprang into Anya's mind of a doctor at Heathfield who, unable to withstand the pressures of overwork and long hours, had become addicted to pethidine. He had obtained the drug for his own use by booking it out to a non-existent patient. He had been found out, severely reprimanded and sent to a rehabilitation centre for treatment. Could it be? No, not Simon. It was impossible. Whatever else he was no addict.

Anya rubbed a trembling hand across her forehead. How could she bear it? And for how long could she cope with the pressure of being forced to suspect the man she loved and admired of such despicable actions?

Then a thought occurred and she slammed the drawer shut and pulled open the bottom one. The treatment sheet was there, filed under 'deceased'. Wang Cheung had died that same evening of oesophageal cancer.

Anya closed the drawer gently, letting out her breath in a long, shaky sigh of relief and walked back into the dispensary. She picked up the second box. The seal was unbroken, the date within the code. She checked the third and the fourth. They, too, were correct. As she picked up the fifth box, her attention was already on the next drug on the shelf. But something was wrong. The box felt light, too light, and when she looked closer she saw the seal had been carefully cut through with either a razor blade or a scalpel.

Anya opened the box. It was empty. Of the five

ampoules of heroin powder it should have contained, there was no sign. With numb fingers she replaced the lid and looked at the code stamped on it. It was earlier than the others. That box should have been at the front, not the back. It was the box that had gone missing. But she had noticed and mentioned it and someone, whoever had taken the ampoules, had replaced the empty box, hoping to delay the discovery of the theft.

Oh God, what was she to do? The obvious move was to tell Simon. But what if he was responsible? He had the only key. He had told her she was mistaken, that nothing was missing. He had checked and said all the boxes were present and correct. But if he *was* responsible, then why had he sent her to check the cupboard? He must have known she'd find the empty box. Was that his intention? Could he be testing her? Waiting to see how she would react? What she would say or do? But *why*? He couldn't know what Charles had told her. Though if he *was* trading in drugs, nothing Charles said would matter anyway. Still, it didn't make sense. One box of diamorphine ampoules wasn't worth that much, even on the black market. Why would Simon risk so much for so little?

Feeling sick, her pulse pounding in her ears, Anya slumped down on the stool, pushing the boxes aside as she buried her head in her hands.

'What are you doing?' Carol's voice, a shocked whisper, roused her and she swung round.

'Dr Brody wants the codes checked,' Anya replied automatically to the question, then stopped as she realised the nurse had no right to ask. Looking at her more carefully, Anya saw that Carol was deathly pale and visibly shaking.

'You know, don't you,' Carol muttered hoarsely. 'You found the empty box.'

Bewildered, Anya nodded slowly and Carol clasped her arms across her chest, hugging herself as if cold. 'That's that, then,' she murmured. 'I'm glad in a way. I couldn't have gone on with it much longer, I don't care what he threatened.' Her face crumpled and tears poured down her wan cheeks as she sagged against the bench, one hand covering her eyes as the other fumbled for a handkerchief.

Anya gasped. 'You mean it was *you* who took the heroin?'

Sobbing, Carol nodded.

'Who threatened you?' Anya demanded. 'And what with?'

'My husband,' Carol gulped. 'He—he——' She couldn't go on.

'But—I didn't know—you said you were single,' Anya was confused. 'I'd better fetch Dr Brody,' she said quietly. She was utterly drained. She had felt too much, too deeply. She had soared to ecstasy and plunged to despair, with jealousy, disillusion and anger thrown in. She wasn't capable of feeling anything, even relief, right now. Simon would have to handle this. After all, as Administrator of the F.C.S. the theft of drugs by a nurse was his problem.

'No,' Carol begged. 'Please—I don't—I can't face Dr Brody.'

'Oh, I'm sure he'll understand,' Anya couldn't hide her bitterness as Charles's accusation leaped into her mind. At once she felt ashamed. Carol was a good nurse. Her reaction to discovery showed she had acted under enormous pressure and dire threats. Besides, didn't her confession absolve Simon from suspicion, at least here on the boat? And it was only Charles's word that the rest was true.

Anya got up and pushed the stool towards the nurse. 'Sit down and tell me how this all came about,' she invited, handing the nurse a wad of tissues.

Carol choked back her sobs and blew her nose. She sank down on to the stool and fiddling with the corner of a tissue gave a watery smile. 'This will cost me my job, I know that, but I'm glad it's all over. I couldn't have gone on, I . . .' Her voice quavered and she lowered her head, struggling for control. 'My parents didn't like Rick, my husband, they said he wasn't—right—for me.'

'What does your husband do for a living?' Anya realised the girl would need gentle prompting to get her thoughts in order.

'He plays bass guitar and sings, with a rock band. They're not one of the big groups, but they get quite a bit of work in the bars and clubs.' She took a deep breath. 'I'd never met anyone like him. I don't know what he saw in me. He'd had lots of girls. There are always plenty hanging around rock groups, willing to do anything.' She looked down as a painful blush flooded her face.

'So you married him against your parents' wishes,' Anya prompted.

Carol nodded. 'I didn't know what else to do.' Her voice was little more than a whisper. 'I was pregnant. Rick didn't know, I hadn't told him. He wanted us to get married. I think he saw us as a sort of Romeo and Juliet, the two of us against the world.'

'What happened when he found out about the baby?'

'He went mad. He told me to get rid of it. He said it wasn't his, that I'd tricked him. He accused me of——' She broke off and wiped her nose again. 'I'd never been with anyone but him. I loved him.' She sounded bewildered, and despite her own confusion and unhappiness Anya's heart went out to the thin, tense girl beside her. 'It all went downhill from there.' Carol swallowed. 'He began staying out all night, and not coming home for days at a time. I was working at the private hospital on Pokfulam, but I had dreadful morning sickness and as soon as the pregnancy began to show, I had to leave. We'd been living in my flat but my savings soon ran out and Rick refused to give me any money, so I had to move to a smaller place in a different area.'

Anya had no doubt that the move had been a big step down from anything Carol had been used to. 'Didn't your parents know what was happening?'

Carol shook her head. 'We'd had a terrible row the week before I got married. I told them I was old enough to know my own mind, that it was my life and I intended to live it my way—and a lot more in the same vein. I couldn't go back and tell them what a fool I'd been.' Another tear slid down her nose and dripped on to the back of her hand as her fingers shredded one of the tissues.

'Who looks after the baby while you're at work?' Anya asked.

'A neighbour. She's Chinese and has a young baby of her own, and is very glad of the money. But what with the cost of food, and clothes and rent, it's going to take months before I can afford the operation.'

Anya was startled. 'What operation? For you?'

Carol shook her head again. 'No, for Helen, my daughter. She has an angioma on her left cheek. When she was born the doctor said it might disappear without treatment, but she's almost a year old and it's shown no sign of fading. It won't be long before she's old enough to wonder why people stare, and the other children will laugh or call her names and I won't have that. But the public hospitals are too busy, so she'll have to go privately. I've been saving as hard as I can, but it's taking so long.' She looked up at Anya. 'It's all my fault,' she whispered.

Anya took the girl's hand in both of hers and squeezed it. 'Don't be silly,' she said briskly. 'You're a nurse, you know perfectly well a strawberry birthmark is simply a collection of tiny blood vessels. It is not a mark of Satan or a punishment for wrongdoing or any other of those ridiculous superstitions.' Anya was beginning to realise what appalling pressure the young nurse must have been under. All this worry and no one to share it with, doing a demanding job and on top of that distorted feelings of guilt that she was somehow responsible for her baby's deformity. 'Why didn't you tell Dr Brody? Why struggle on alone all this time?'

'He would have fired me. I had to lie to get the job. The F.C.S. doesn't employ nurses with young children because of the uncertain hours and overnight stops. Dr Brody couldn't have made an exception for me and, if I'd lost the job, I couldn't possibly have got another that paid as well, and Helen's operation would have had to wait even longer. That was what Rick was holding over me. Once he found out about my job he threatened to expose me to Dr Brody, anonymously of course, if I didn't give him the drugs he wanted. It wasn't for me.' She clutched Anya's arm. 'You have to believe that, I did it for Helen.'

'Is you husband an addict?' Anya asked gently.

Carol nodded. 'I think so. I think he sells drugs as well.'

Anya stood up and drew Carol to her feet. The nurse looked exhausted and utterly beaten. 'Go and wash your face, have a cup of coffee, then carry on with your work. I'm going to see Dr Brody. We'll work something out so try not to worry.'

Carol's chin quivered. 'You've been so kind.'

'Do you have any brothers or sisters?' Anya asked suddenly.

Surprised, Carol shook her head. 'No, why?'

'Your parents are doubtless angry and upset and it will take courage for you to face them and admit you made a wrong choice. But everyone makes mistakes, it's a necessary part of life, of growing up. But you've got something very special on your side, something that will make that first meeting much easier.'

Carol frowned, puzzled. 'What's that?'

Anya smiled. 'Their first grandchild.' She went to the door.

'Dr Lucas.' Anya turned to see the nurse holding out her hand. Something metallic glinted on her palm.

'What is it?'

'A key to the C.D. cupboard. I—I had a duplicate made. That's how I was able to get—you'd better have it now.'

Anya nodded, took the key and went to find Simon.

# CHAPTER EIGHT

'SHE—what?' Simon roared. Anya flinched but stood her ground. So stretched were her own nerves that her initial impulse was to shout back, but she managed to hold her voice steady and remain calm as she recounted Carol's story. 'This was the second box of diamorphine ampoules she had taken.'

'The second?' Simon snapped. 'When did she take the first, and why wasn't it missed?'

'The week before I arrived. It was a box you were sending back to the Pharmacy because of damage. Two of the ampoules were cracked. Instead of handing it in, Carol kept it. That was when she took an impression of your key and had a duplicate made.'

Simon's expression was stony and his eyes were twin flames.

'The girl has been under tremendous pressure,' Anya added quickly. 'She's a good nurse, quick and conscientious, and being forced to do something so totally against her upbringing and training must have been intolerable. On top of all this, she'll now lose her job, which will create even more difficulties for her.'

'If things are as bad as you say,' he interrupted brusquely, 'she's not fit to be working anyway.' He went towards the door. 'You had better get back to the dispensary.'

Anya was bewildered. 'Where are you going? Surely we ought to sort this out, decide what to do.'

'I already have,' he interrupted again. 'We're only a couple of hours out of Victoria, less than halfway to the settlement. I'm radioing for the Harbour Police. I want that girl off this boat as soon as possible.'

Deeply shaken, Anya tried to call him back, 'No, Simon, wait—you can't——' she cried urgently, but he had already gone.

Carol was chalk-white but reasonably composed as she brought her suitcase from the cabin and set it down just inside the consulting room. The two uniformed policemen stood either side of the door.

Susan's plump face was aghast as she stared at the girl she had shared a cabin with for six months, who had not in all that time let slip a single word about her problems and unhappiness. She ran forward and seized Carol's hands. 'Why?' She demanded. 'Why didn't you tell me? Maybe I could have helped in some way.'

Carol was already shaking her head, trying to smile at her friend. 'It would have put you in an impossible situation, Sue, I couldn't do that to you.' She lowered her voice. 'Give Kam-Li my best wishes for a speedy recovery.' She pressed Susan's hand. 'I hope everything works out well for you both. You're very lucky, he's a good, honest . . .' Her smile faltered and she disengaged her hands and turned to Simon. 'There's not much I can say, Dr Brody. I lied to get this job, I've betrayed your trust.'

Anya looked up at Simon. Surely he must see the girl was not a criminal through choice? She had done those things out of sheer desperation, not knowing which way to turn. But his face was an expressionless mask. Nowhere could she see any trace of sympathy or understanding. How could he be so cold? How could he hand this girl over to the police without a trace of compassion?

She couldn't let it happen. If she did not do something, say something, she would never forgive herself.

If what Charles had told her was true, Simon had no right to stand in judgment on the young nurse, who had done what she did for her baby, out of fear, not for monetary gain. *If* it was true. She would not accuse him. She could not do that. But nor could she simply stand by while he sent Carol to jail.

Simon caught her eye. Forgive me, my love, she pleaded silently, and took a deep breath.

Something moved behind his eyes, an expression so fleeting she could not read it clearly. But she had an overriding impression of hurt, of anger, disappointment and *hurt*. Before she could say anything, to her complete amazement, Simon went over to Carol, and put his arm around her shoulders, speaking to her alone, although everyone else could hear what was said.

'You're quite sure what you told Dr Lucas was the truth? Nothing omitted?'

'As God is my witness, Dr Brody.' Carol turned anxious eyes up to Simon.

'All right.' He cut her off gently. 'These officers will see you safely home. As from today you are on paid sick leave. I'll arrange for another agency nurse to replace you for the time being. You are to rest, eat properly and spend time with your baby. Is that understood?'

Utterly stunned, Carol gazed at him for a long moment, then her eyes brimmed and she nodded.

One of the policemen stepped forward. 'About charges, sir——'

'I am bringing no charges against this young woman, officer,' Simon said firmly. 'But she will need police protection until her husband has been tried and convicted. Can you arrange that?'

'Yes sir. Of course it would be most helpful if we could count on the young lady's assistance in our enquiries. A statement, identification, that sort of thing.'

Simon raised an eyebrow at Carol. 'Will you help them?'

She nodded. 'Yes.' Her voice was low but steady.

'Right, sir.' The other policeman picked up Carol's suitcase. 'If there's nothing further, we'll be——'

'Just a moment,' Anya interrupted, her heart hammering as relief and gratitude surged through her. She snatched up a notepad. 'Can someone lend me a pen?' The nearer of the policemen handed her a ballpoint and resting the pad on the table she leaned over and began writing furiously.

'I presume this is important?' Simon enquired coolly.

'Yes.' She didn't look up. As soon as she had finished she tore off the sheet, folded it and gave it to Carol. 'Take this to Doctor Charles Hagen at the Private Hospital on Pokfulam Road, He's reputed to be one of the best plastic surgeons in the colony, so your baby should be in good hands.'

'But . . .' Carol looked at the note Anya had thrust into her hand, 'I can't afford——'

'It won't cost you a cent, I promise,' Anya reassured her, and handed back the policeman's pen with a smile of thanks.

Carol's eyes filled up again. 'Thank you, all of you,' she whispered. 'I wish . . .' She broke off with a helpless gesture and hurried out into the corridor, the policemen following.

After the launch had gone, bouncing away over the grey waves, Anya returned to the theatre. She wanted to talk to Simon, to tell him how much she appreciated his gentle handling of Carol, and how she had misjudged his apparent coldness, seeing it as accusation not objectivity.

She pushed open the swing doors, a smile of apology ready on her lips. He looked up from the suction apparatus he was testing with a glance so cold and forbidding it sent a shiver of fear through her. Her smile died. Simon gave her no chance to speak. 'As we're one nurse short for the remainder of this trip, I'd be obliged if you would complete the code check on the rest of the preparations in the dispensary.'

'Yes, of course,' Anya said, then hesitated, her glance flicking to Susan who, apparently deep in her own thoughts, was folding operating towels and drapes for the steriliser.

'Well?' He was utterly unapproachable. She had never seen him like this. There was an icy bitterness about him that terrified her. She backed out of the theatre and returned to the dispensary. What had happened? What had caused the sudden change in him?

The rest of the day passed in a blur. When she went for lunch Susan was just finishing hers and hurried away with a murmured apology. She still had some of Carol's work to finish. Simon didn't show up at all and Anya didn't know whether to be glad or sorry.

As she returned to the dispensary she noticed the boat was beginning to pitch and roll. The bad weather was coming in faster than expected. But even the threat of another typhoon did not unnerve her as much as Simon's sudden and total withdrawal.

She worked on through the afternoon, fighting a losing battle to concentrate on what she was doing. And the realisation broke over her with shattering force of just how much she loved Simon. For good or ill, for better or worse, no matter what he was supposed to have done, she would always love him. She had been so stunned by Charles's revelations she had fled from Simon, not knowing how to face him, but now he was rejecting her and it hurt more than she could ever have believed possible.

The atmosphere at the evening meal was electric. Susan attempted to open a conversation once or twice, but after being met with either a blank stare or a brief, preoccupied mutter, gave up and after finishing her meal excused herself, saying she had letters to write.

Anya and Simon were alone for the first time that day, the debris of their meal littering the table. The pitch and roll of the boat was growing greater by the minute as the Captain battled to get them to the settlement and a safe anchorage before nightfall.

The tension was unbearable. Anya pushed back her chair and stood up. At once Simon did the same, his tall figure between her and the door.

Anya could feel colour mounting in her face. She clung to the table as the boat plunged into a trough then heaved itself out again.

Trepidation fluttered inside her like moths' wings.

Balanced on the balls of his feet, swaying easily with the seesawing motion of the boat, Simon looked immovable. Behind him the cook came in to clear the table. Simon stepped aside to let the Chinese pass and Anya seized her opportunity to escape. But Simon's hand snaked out and grasped her upper arm with a firmness that bordered on pain.

'Let me go,' Anya hissed, pulling away from him. 'I—I've got work to do.'

'Not tonight,' he said. 'Tonight we talk.'

'All right, we'll talk,' she agreed trying to hide her apprehension while her heart sang at his touch. 'Shall we stay here, or do you prefer the consulting room?'

His mouth widened in a humourless smile. 'Nice and impersonal, is that the idea? It won't wash, Anya. We are going where we won't be disturbed for the whole night, where there's no place for you to hide.'

And before she could protest he was marching her along the passage to their cabin.

Thrusting her inside, he followed locking the door and leaning against it. 'Now, I want to know what the hell is going on?'

Anya spun round. In the gloom Simon was a towering black shape against the door.

'*You* want to know?' She fumbled for the nearest light, the one over his bunk. She pressed the switch and a soft glow filled the small cabin. She turned back, trying to dredge up anger. 'You're the one acting like some heavy in a third-rate film.'

'Cut it out, Anya,' he warned softly and she shivered.

'I don't know what you mean, honestly,' she added quickly as his eyes narrowed.

He took a step towards her. 'Did you enjoy our time together yesterday?' he asked quietly. 'The meal we had, our sightseeing, the temple and Tiger Balm Gardens?'

The question took her completely by surprise and her expression softened, her lips turning up at the corners as warm memories of all they had done and seen swept over her. 'Oh yes,' she murmured.

'Then Hagen turned up and carted you off for the evening and when you got back you were, to put it mildly, upset. Since then not only have you treated me like a plague carrier, you send a note to Hagen and inform Carol that he will operate on her baby free, on your say-so. Now I know enough about Charles Hagen to be quite certain he wouldn't give anyone a cold if he could charge for it, so just what is going on? Why should he do you any favours?'

Anya sat down on the nearest bunk, past caring that it was Simon's. 'No, you've got it all wrong, it's nothing like that.'

'Nothing like what?'

'What you're implying, that Charles and I . . .' Anya's face was burning. 'Charles was drunk. He tried to kiss me and I fought him off. He rang this morning to apologise. He wanted to make amends. The best way he can do that is to operate on Carol's baby. That's what I said in the note.'

'That's all there is to it?' Simon was relentless.

'Of course, that's all,' Anya flared.

'I don't believe you,' Simon said flatly. 'You were far more upset than a brief scrimmage with a drunken boyfriend warranted.'

Anya jumped to her feet, but, as he had promised, there was nowhere to run. Simon had pushed himself away from the door. Tall, powerful, he seemed to fill the cabin. Anya stepped back and the edge of the bunk caught her behind the knees and she fell on to it. Scrambling backwards against the wall she drew her legs up beneath her, trying to get away from him.

Simon looked down at her. 'Stop lying to me, Anya,' he grated. Then without warning he sat down on the bunk, half-turned towards her and ran a hand through his rumpled black hair. 'For God's sake, tell me the truth, the whole truth.' Unable to escape, forced to listen, for the first time Anya heard the note of pleading in his voice. 'Give me that much at least. If it wasn't Hagen's kisses that upset you, it had to be something else.'

'He didn't—do—anything else,' Anya broke in.

'Then it had to be something he said, and from the way you've behaved since last last night, it had to be something about me.' He turned his head and their eyes met.

Anya could only stare at him. This was her chance. She could bring it out into the open now. She could face him with Charles's accusations and he'd have to answer.

But the words would not come. Charles had sworn Simon was guilty. And if Simon admitted it, what then? How would she cope with the knowledge? She loved him, nothing would alter that, yet if he confirmed what Charles had said, how could she stay silent? But could she inform on him? Be the one to destroy all he had built? No doubt the F.C.S. would continue without him, but it could never ever be the same. And what would happen to Pixie? To Madam Sen? To those for whom he was so much more than just 'the doctor'? She couldn't do it.

He throat was dry and her tongue stuck to the roof of her mouth. She tried to moisten her lips. 'No,' she began, 'you're wrong.'

He shook his head. 'Don't you understand?' he demanded softly. 'I heard. When Hagen brought you home last night in a screech of brakes, I came out, just to make sure you were all right. He's got the reputation of driving like a maniac. Then I heard the car door. You didn't shut it, you slammed it, hard. I was curious, I admit it. I was also—concerned. I had no intention of interfering.' The shadow of a smile played across his mouth. 'You're a determined and capable woman, and I guessed you could handle Hagen, but I wanted to be around—just in case.' The smile vanished and in the lamplight his features were suddenly vulnerable. 'I heard what Hagen said, and ever since then I've been waiting for you to tell me.'

'How could I?' Anya cried.

'You don't know whether to believe him or not, do you.' Simon made the remark a statement.

Anya shook her head briefly, she felt utterly wretched.

'I thought that we were—friends, that you had faith in me.'

Each word cut like a knife into Anya's soul. 'We are, and I do,' she whispered, her throat tight.

'Yet you avoided me. You said nothing. Oh, you were going to once, when I was about to send Carol ashore with the police. God alone knows *what* you'd have said, but——'

'I'd have had to,' Anya cried, 'you seemed so cold, so impassive. That girl was suffering——'

'So was I,' he blazed, 'and not over Carol.' Anya's eyes flew wide with shock. He lunged forward and seized her arms. 'Don't I even get a chance to defend myself? Don't you care enough to want to know the truth? Anya, do I mean anything at all to you?'

She stared at him. Did he really not know? She recalled the temple, the fragrance of incense and her silent prayer that he might love her. Could it possibly be he had been suffering over *her*? She relived the deep, satisfying pleasure of working alongside him, of listening to him and learning as he talked. Then her memory was flooded with images; his head bent over hers, his bronzed, naked body separated from hers by only a thin cotton sheet as only two nights ago, in this very cabin he had caressed her, the taste of his kisses, the agony of longing she had suffered, and the fear of its fulfilment.

Tears sparkled and hovered on her lashes then spilled over to trickle slowly down her cheeks. 'Do you mean anything?' She choked on the words and burying her face in her hands began to laugh helplessly.

She felt herself dragged forward into his arms and cradled against his chest. Gently he pushed her hands aside, wiping away her tears with his forefinger, his look of perplexity fading as realisation and wonder spread across his features. Then in a single, sweeping movement he lay her down on the bunk, her back to the bulkhead, and stretched out beside her, leaning on one elbow.

'No!' Anya began, trying to struggle upright, but he laid a finger on her lips.

'Sssh,' he murmured, 'don't worry. First things first. There must be no more doubts or suspicions, no more fear, of any kind. Ask the question, Anya.'

Outside the wind shrieked and howled. The boat rolled and tossed as it lurched towards its destination. Anya looked up into Simon's eyes. His gaze was open and guileless. From somewhere far away she heard her own voice. 'Your house—your money—are they the proceeds of drug running?'

'Yes,' he stated quietly. Anya flinched as though he had slapped her. 'But not in the way Hagen intended you to think. What he said was true, but it was distorted, manipulated truth.'

'I—I don't understand.'

'It's a long story,' Simon warned.

Anya managed a tiny smile. 'I'm not going anywhere.'

Simon rested his head on his folded arm and took one of Anya's hands in his as they lay facing one another. 'My great-grandfather was one of the first British merchants to come to Hong Kong. He and his cronies were trying to sell opium to the Chinese.'

Anya's eyes widened. 'What? But I thought——'

'Yes,' Simon's tone was ironic, 'everyone has heard of Chinese opium dens, but few people realise it was the British, with their Victorian morality and ideals and their commercial interests in India, who actually established and built up the drug trade.'

'But didn't the Chinese try to stop them?'

'Of course. The government in Peking organised a siege on factories processing the drug, then appointed a special commissioner to confiscate all the opium in Canton, the distribution point.'

'I don't suppose that went down very well.'

'It didn't. The British Superintendent of Trade withdrew all the British merchants and their families on to ships anchored in the harbour, which brought commerce to a virtual standstill. Then he demanded that China refund the value of the seized opium and guarantee the safety of British traders.'

'What was China's reaction?'

'They said no.'

'What happened then?' Anya prompted, fascinated by what Simon was telling her.

'With less than three thousand men the British attacked and seized the commercial centres of Amoy, Ningpo, Foochow and Shanghai. To save Nangking which was next on the list, China surrendered. They agreed to pay for the opium and to allow British merchants and consuls to reside in the four captured cities. But most important, they handed over Hong Kong Island to the British.'

'Good Lord,' Anya breathed, 'it's like something out of a pirate film.'

'It was real enough,' Simon replied grimly. 'By nineteen-hundred opium was providing one-sixth of Hong Kong's revenue. It wasn't outlawed until after the Second World War.'

'What happened to your great-grandfather?'

'Like so many rogues, he prospered,' Simon smiled drily. 'He used the money he'd made from opium to establish legitimate trading interests. My grandfather followed him into the business and built the house on Bay View.'

'Your house?' Anya asked.

He nodded. 'My grandfather was a strange old man, but very perceptive. When he died he left equal amounts of money to all his grandchildren except me. He left me his house. The others all sympathised. No cash, just a pile of bricks and mortar which if I'd sold it wouldn't have fetched as much as they received.' Simon smiled, remembering.

'Why did he do that?' Anya was enthralled by the history Simon was unfolding, and by the pleasure of learning more about him and his family background.

'I lived with my grandparents for quite a while as a child. My mother died when I was six,' he said with a brevity Anya sensed hid the still vivid memory of a child's grief and sense of loss. 'My father married again a couple of years later and he and my stepmother spent much of the year abroad on business, mainly in America. So, I stayed with my grandparents. My grandfather was a hard businessman, but there was also a touch of the artist about him, and being singularly unimpressed by the gothic monstrosities his contemporaries were erecting, he had the house built according to the ancient Chinese tradition that a dwelling should harmonise with its surroundings, not stand out from them. He knew how much I grew to love that place, its serenity, its sense of timelessness. He gave me something money couldn't buy.' He raised her hand to his lips and kissed it tenderly. 'You know what I'm talking about. You love it, too.' It was a statement, not a question, but his eyes demanded an answer.

Anya swallowed, and nodded once. Simon had laid the ghost of Charles's accusations. Anya could see now how Charles, inflamed by jealousy, spite and too much alcohol, had twisted the truth so that the drug-running on which Simon's great-grandfather had founded his business over one hundred years ago, had been made to sound like Simon's crime. Even this morning on the 'phone, Charles had still insisted Simon was guilty. Was that because of Kerry?

It all came back to Kerry. With his last few words,

Simon had destroyed her fragile cocoon of peace and contentment. He was right. She did love the house. But as soon as they returned she would have to leave it. It was ridiculous how much the thought upset her. She had never felt the slightest attachment to any of the other places she had lived in. But this was Simon's house, and he loved it, and she loved him. She wrenched her eyes from his, afraid he might somehow read her thoughts. For though one barrier between them had been removed, another still remained, and about that she could do nothing.

But while they were here, on the boat, in the cabin, she could pretend. Let the dream continue a while longer. She wanted him to go on talking, so that she could listen, learn about him, watch that beloved mouth while he spoke, to lie beside him perhaps for the last time.

'Did you do your training out here?' she asked softly.

He shook his head. 'At St Thomas's and the London School of Hygiene and Tropical Medicine. London was fascinating, but English weather . . .' He grimaced.

Anya grinned. 'In case you hadn't noticed, there's a typhoon blowing outside, and you have the nerve to complain about *English* weather?'

Simon scowled at her, then brought her hand to his lips once more, kissing each of her fingers as though they were infinitely precious.

The pressure of his mouth was a high voltage current, charging her with sudden, vibrant life. Warm colour flushed her throat and rose like a tide to her cheeks. Anya struggled to retain her composure. 'What brought you back here? Didn't you want to see more of the world?'

'During my training I had spent some time in

America,' he acknowledged, and settled his head more comfortably on his arm, moving fractionally closer to Anya. 'Considering my family background, it was unavoidable that I should grow up with the idea that a man is measured by his wealth and power.' Anya had a vivid mental image of Charles, glass in hand, leaning back at their table in the Hong Kong Hilton. 'That's how you're judged,' he had said, 'that's how society labels the successes and failures. It's all in the bank balance.'

'And in the States,' Simon went on, 'medicine really is big business. The hospitals are profit-making organisations. The pressures on doctors are horrendous and spill over into social life. Alcoholism is widespread and coke-sniffing almost obligatory. I got sick of watching supposedly intelligent people who had undergone years of medical training, destroying their health and their lives. Besides,' his tone softened, 'this is my home. Poverty and disease in the colony are rife. We can't do much about the poverty, but in our small way, the F.C.S. is doing something to fight disease. Which reminds me, I need your help.'

'Mine?' Anya was startled and delighted. 'In what way?'

'I want to enlist Madam Sen's help to persuade Pixie's parents to face the truth, that their little girl does have leprosy, but that it is the milder type and with regular treatment she will be completely cured.'

'That's a great idea,' Anya nodded, 'but why do you need my help?'

'Madame Sen took to you, she was willing to talk, to describe her life, her past, some of what she had been through.'

'Has she never said those things to you?' Anya asked.

'Some of them,' he admitted, 'but I sensed she found

it difficult. My being a doctor wasn't always enough to overcome her natural reticence in revealing so much to a man. Yet it wasn't simply the fact of your being a woman or even a female doctor that got her to open up. There was an empathy between you.'

Anya nodded. 'I thought so, too, but I was afraid it was just my imagination, or wishful thinking. I'm glad you noticed, because I've had an idea as well. Simon, she was born into a lifestyle the villagers have never even heard of. She travelled all over the world, then because of her illness, was forced to leave behind everything she had ever known and learn to cope with an entirely different way of life. She has seen and experienced more than most people could cram into three lifetimes.' Anya paused, then announced almost defiantly, 'I think she'd make an excellent teacher, not in the conventional sense maybe, but the school would benefit enormously from her experience, her knowledge. She's too fine a person and she has too much to give to waste the rest of her life looking after ducks and chickens.'

Simon studied her, his amber gaze deep and penetrating in the soft glow of the lamp. 'You're absolutely right,' he said at last, and Anya's cheeks were suffused with rosy warmth. He squeezed the hand imprisoned in his own. 'We make a pretty good partnership, you and I,' he smiled.

Anya looked away quickly, not wanting him to see the joy and anguish that knifed through her. She struggled to sit up, but he pushed her down again, leaning over her as she fell back on to the pillow. 'I haven't finished, Anya,' he growled. 'I know this is a bit sudden,' he shrugged helplessly, 'God knows I wasn't expecting it to happen quite so——' He broke off, seemed to search for the right words and began again. 'We work well together, far better than I ever imagined we would, but it's not enough, Anya, I want more than that.'

'No.' She shook her head violently, pushing against his chest, trying to wriggle out from under him. 'No, no,' she kept repeating, denying her own longing as she tried to convince them both.

He held her down with ease, unaware of his own strength, his tanned features clouded with bewilderment. 'But I thought—now you know the truth about what Hagen said——'

'It's got nothing to do with that,' Anya panted. 'Will you let me go?'

'No,' came the flat reply. 'Why are you acting like this? There is something special between us, I know it and so do you.'

'My feelings are my own business,' she thrashed about furiously, 'and regardless of what *you* want I'm afraid a *ménage à trois* is not my scene. I've never pretended to be *that* sophisticated.'

'A—what?' he spluttered, amazement creasing his forehead.

'You heard,' she cried. 'First Kerry, now me. How many more are you planning to coax into your bed?' She could have bitten off her tongue. She was trying to show she didn't care and making it all too plain that she did. 'Of course it's none of my business,' she said quickly, stifling the sharp pangs of jealousy.

Then, to her bewilderment, Simon began to smile. A chuckle started deep in his throat and erupted in a burst of laughter that confused Anya.

'What's so funny?' she demanded in a small voice, suddenly unsure of herself.

'Now I see why you were so anxious to leave when I said Kerry was coming home,' he spoke softly, still smiling, but with a tenderness in his expression that made her heart leap. 'Oh, Anya, you sweet idiot.

Kerry is my stepsister. She lives at my house when my father and stepmother are abroad. Ah Mai looks after her and I can discourage potential fortune-hunters. She's been in Switzerland for three months on a language course.'

Anya was totally still. 'Your stepsister?' she repeated.

He nodded, stroking the tousled curls from her forehead. 'She's nineteen, and thinks I'm an old man. For the last three years she and Ah Mai have been trying to marry me off to a succession of the most unsuitable women.' He bent and brushed his lips across hers. 'You can put a stop to all that nonsense.' He kissed her again, still gentle, but lingering, and his grip tightened as Anya clutched convulsively at his shoulders as relief, joy and the realisation of what he was saying exploded within her. He raised his head. 'There are no more skeletons rattling the family closet,' he put one hand over his heart, 'I swear it.'

'Good,' Anya smiled up at him and lifted her hand to touch his face, tracing the line of his jaw with her fingertips.

'And no just cause or impediment why we should not be joined together as man and wife?' He spoke lightly, almost mockingly, but the look in his eyes revealed the depth of his feelings.

'None.' She met his gaze, no longer afraid, no longer hiding the love that had transformed her life in such a short time, causing her more agony and ecstasy than she had ever dreamed of.

'You're the woman I've waited for,' he said softly, cupping her head in his hands. 'You're the part of me that was missing. I love you, Anya.' He drew her close, his body melding with hers, and she came to him willingly, joyfully, and their kiss lasted a long time.

When they broke apart, breathless, hearts racing, a

thought occurred to Anya. 'What about Ah Mai? Will she mind?'

Simon didn't let her finish. 'Ah Mai has already stated her intention of being *amah* to our babies,' he said drily. 'I sometimes think that woman is a witch. She made that announcement the day I brought you home.'

Anya hugged him, her cheeks flushing as she recalled the little woman's smiling wrinkled face and bright, boot-button eyes.

'Simon, listen.' Anya lay perfectly still, concentrating. 'I can't hear the wind, and the boat isn't pitching any more. Has the typhoon passed?'

He shook his head. 'No, my love. It's still raging out there, but we've reached our safe harbour,' and he reached up and turned off the lamp.

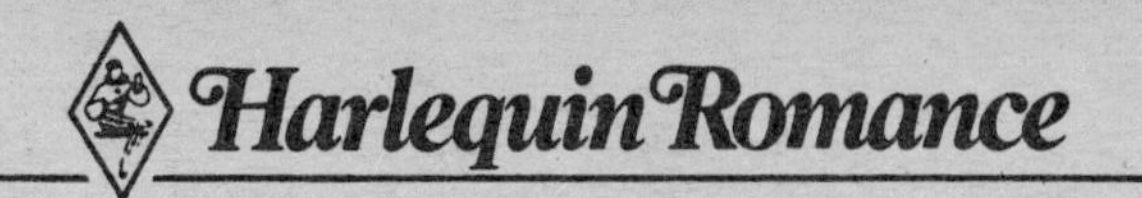

## Coming Next Month

**#2965 NO GREATER JOY Rosemary Carter**
Alison fights hard against her attraction to Clint, driven by bitter memories of a past betrayal. However, handsome, confident, wealthy Clint Demaine isn't a man to take no for an answer.

**#2966 A BUSINESS ARRANGEMENT Kate Denton**
When Lauren advertises for a husband interested in a business-like approach to marriage, she doesn't expect a proposal from a handsome Dallas attorney. If only love were part of the bargain....

**#2967 THE LATIMORE BRIDE Emma Goldrick**
Mattie Latimore expects problems—supervising a lengthy engineering project in the Sudan is going to be a daunting experience. Yet heat, desert and hostile African tribes are nothing compared to the challenge of Ryan Quinn. (More about the Latimore family introduced in THE ROAD and TEMPERED BY FIRE.)

**#2968 MODEL FOR LOVE Rosemary Hammond**
Felicia doesn't want to get involved with handsome financial wizard Adam St. John—he reminds her of the man who once broke her heart. So she's leery of asking him to let her sculpt him—it might just be playing with fire!

**#2969 CENTREFOLD Valerie Parv**
Helping her twin sister out of a tight spot seems no big deal to Danni—until she learns she's supposed to deceive Rowan Traynor, her sister's boyfriend. When he discovers the switch his reaction is a complete surprise to Danni....

**#2970 THAT DEAR PERFECTION Alison York**
A half share in a Welsh perfume factory is a far cry from Sophie usual job as a model, but she looks on it as an exciting challenge. It is unfortunate that Ben Ross, her new partner, looks on Sophie as a gold digger.

Available in March wherever paperback books are sold, or through Harlequin Reader Service:

| In the U.S. | In Canada |
|---|---|
| 901 Fuhrmann Blvd. | P.O. Box 603 |
| P.O. Box 1397 | Fort Erie, Ontario |
| Buffalo, N.Y. 14240-1397 | L2A 5X3 |

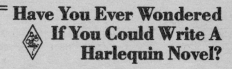